A DEAL WITH THE DEVIL NOVEL

SILHOUETTE

CARIN HART

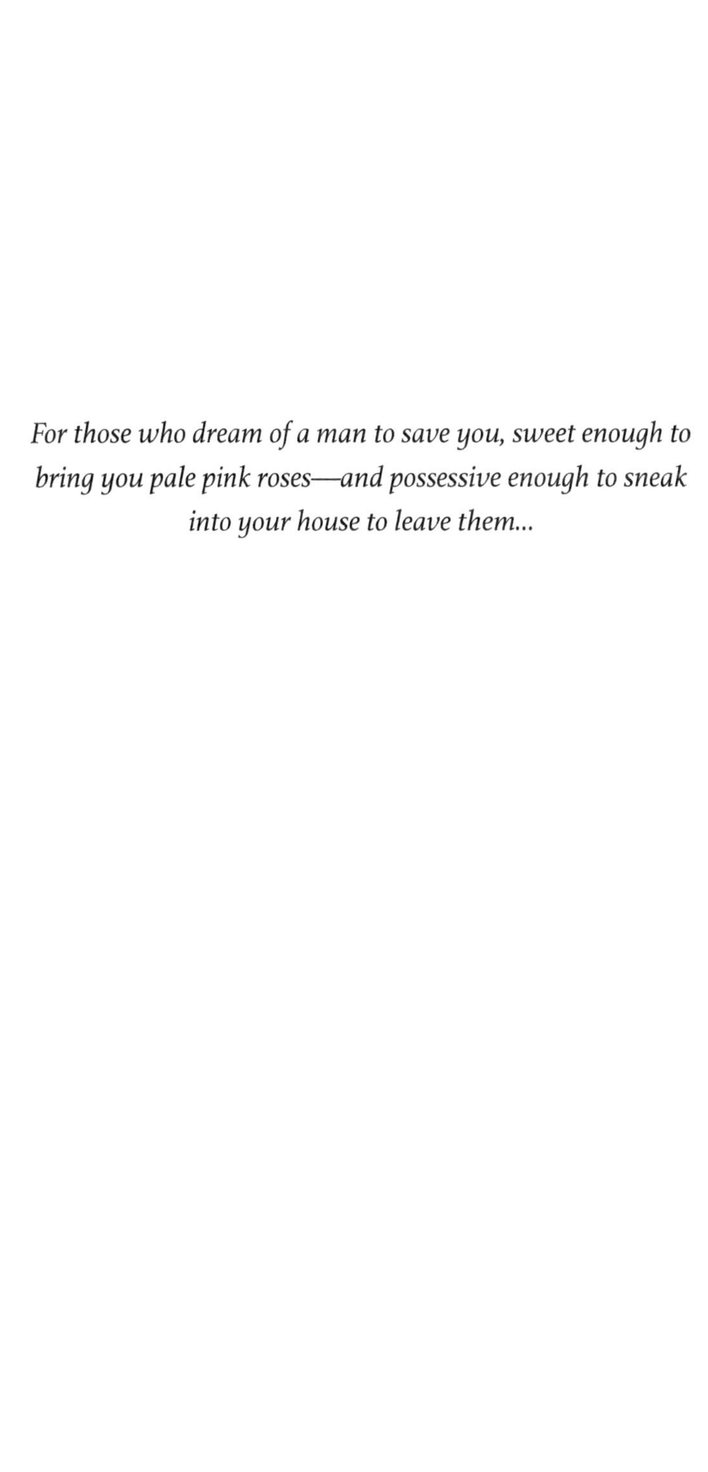

For those who dream of a man to save you, sweet enough to bring you pale pink roses—and possessive enough to sneak into your house to leave them...

PLEASE NOTE

This book is a stalker romance that is part of the **Deal with the Devil** universe. While it's a complete stand-alone (with a HEA), Jake and Simone's romance—or, really, his obsession with her—is a small subplot in *The Devil's Playground.* If you wanted to know more about Royce's deviant younger cousin, Jake, this is his story!

However, while I can guarantee that these characters—like all my others—have a HEA that suits them, this is also a dark romance. As such, I have compiled a list of content warnings.

Silhouette includes: dubcon/CNC, stalking activities (including tracking the FMCs vehicle, putting up cameras, and sneaking into her house), the aftermath of a murder on page (in the prologue), mentions of previous physical/emotional/financial abuse from the FMCs ex-husband, cockwarming, food tampering, drugging, a heroine having an obvious mental health crisis throughout the book, and a masked hero who will push her to her limits while loving her just the way she is.

xoxo,
Carin

PART ONE
BLOODY VALENTINE

"OH MY LOVE.
PLEASE DON'T CRY

I'LL WASH MY BLOODY HANDS.
AND WE'LL START A NEW LIFE..."

Bloody Valentine,
Good Charlotte (2002)

PROLOGUE, PART I

JAKE

never meant to kill William Burke, not really, but as I look down on his corpse, I have only one thought: *try taking Simone from me again, fucker*.

Does it matter that she was his wife first? Not to me. I couldn't save her from marrying this asshole because I didn't know Simone four years ago when she was barely twenty-three and thought it was a good idea to say 'I do'. It's only been a few months since I first saw her, but watching her fight back tears outside of Springfield Stop 'n Go as Will bitched at her for grabbing the wrong size box of condoms... she was mine from that moment on, and all because I've always been a sucker for a pretty blonde with haunted eyes, trapped in a shitty situation, and in need of a knight in shining armor.

In this case, her hero is wearing jeans, a blood-speckled flannel, and the six-mil nitrile gloves I snagged from my new garage as soon as I found out that Burke had followed Simone out of Springfield and all the way to Merrill Grove.

He shouldn't have. I thought the not-so-subtle warnings I'd given him to keep his distance had gotten through his thick skull. The three slashed tires to prevent him from leaving town, or the way I superglued the outer lock to his apartment's front door... but no. The asshole decided to go after Simone again, and this time I was betting he wouldn't back down until she was in the ground—or *he* was.

That's why I'm here now, staring down at the body of a man I never planned on killing, feeling nothing but cold satisfaction that I *did*.

Prick. He made her cry because he thought his cock was bigger than it was, and he refused to accept they were over when she told him she wanted a divorce, then fled from him when his counteroffer was to decorate Simone's pretty face with a black eye so purple, not even her make-up could hide it from me.

I should've killed him then. The only reason I didn't was because I hated the idea that it would fall on Simone. The cops in my home city might be crooked as fuck, but if you don't have connections to the local mafias—the Libellula Family or the Sinners Syndicate—then you're screwed. The Sinners got my back, but

Simone? The shoddy law would go after her, and I didn't have enough pull to protect her after the trouble I got into when I was a kid.

Ah, Heather... Burke isn't the only blood on my hands—my *gloves*—even if he is the first person I've killed myself. Casey could still be alive for all I know, and Heather was a tragedy, but Will Burke?

He thought he could take Simone from me. After I've watched her... after I've claimed her as mine... after I allowed my obsession to consume me so entirely, I built a whole new life—became a brand new Jake McIntyre—in order to keep her for my own... weeks after I already settled in Merrill Grove myself, this bastard entered *my* territory and thought my pretty boy smile and year-younger age meant I was no match for him.

Maybe I wasn't, but my ZT 350 knife sure fucking was.

He only has himself to blame for what happened. After arriving in town late last night before Simone refused to let him inside her new house, he came back to the cul de sac full of short-term rentals early this morning. I was expecting him, but he still caught me doing what I've been doing for weeks now, taking every moment I'm not playing my part down at Frank's Garage to find peace in watching Simone from outside her window, even if he was too self-consumed to realize that I didn't just so happen to be out for an early morning walk when he pulled his car into Simone's driveway.

He didn't recognize me. Not from that day outside of the convenience store, or all the times I tried to get close to the Burkes after that. Delivering food up to their apartment on the quieter side of the city or accidentally shopping for my groceries at the same time Simone was... even parking my ass outside their building with a clipboard and a crooked smile as I asked her to sign some bullshit petition, just to see how she swirled the "S" and dotted the "i" in her name. From the end of December to mid-February, I was always there—but when I waved at him this late March morning, hailing him over to see why he was back at Simone's again in the guise of being just another friendly neighbor, he barely registered I was talking to him.

That's my superpower. I can blend in if I have to, and with a boyish grin on my lips, he never expected I was lying my ass off when I told him Simone had already left for work, but as that friendly neighbor, I could give him instructions to where the fictitious diner she waited tables at was located. And, whoops, Merrill Grove might be a small town about an hour out of Springfield, but it's confusing for even locals, and maybe he'd be better off following behind me since I'm heading that way regardless.

I'm no local. I tracked Simone here two weeks ago, then decided to stay when it was obvious this was no vacation for her. This was her escape, and I'd be there to make sure she pulled it off.

But Burke didn't know that. At least, not until I parked my nondescript sedan in a quiet back alley and he got out of his overpriced luxury car, cursing me out for playing games with his valuable time. Already accepting that there isn't anything I won't do for Simone, I met him midway, my knife hidden in my hand.

I wanted him out of Simone's life. So did she. After what I've learned about her so far, my sweet vixen—deceptively innocent though there's something about her that tempts me to beg her to be *wicked*—isn't the type of woman to expect someone else to handle her problems for her. She'd rather run from them than rely on anyone else or even ask for a hand.

She doesn't have to. Already I know enough about Simone that she'd never ask—but she'll understand that I've done this all for her.

She'll *have* to.

One slice. That's all it took. One stab in the side to get his attention, then one swing with the knife, one slice across his carotid. I didn't hesitate. He proved that he would keep coming back again and again until Simone broke down and let him in—or she ran. She seems to like Merrill Grove. With my new place and a job down at the garage, I'd rather watch her here than start over somewhere else.

And that meant Will Burke had to go.

He gagged on his blood, choking on it, then collapsed to the gravel path behind the abandoned movie theater where I led him. It's sandwiched between a hardware store that went out of business years ago, another business that's an eyesore the locals pretend not to notice.

I'm not worried about being seen, either. Always a planner, I'd been thinking about taking Burke out from the moment I caught sight of his angry face appearing on the cameras I rigged up on Simone's property the morning after I rented this place. This spot was perfectly chosen for me to confront him, and if I never got the chance to warn him away from my sweet vixen, then too fucking bad.

Only as I'm pulling my gloves off, using the plastic to wipe the blood from my blade, do I realize that I'm stuck with a dead body, an extra vehicle, and no idea what to do with either.

I'm twisted. I'm broken. I love too deeply, and I lose all sense of right and wrong, should and shouldn't, sane and batshit crazy whenever I find the one.

I lost Casey.

Heather was never mine.

But Simone?

They say that the third time's the charm, and they better fucking be *right*.

My knife clean, I ball up the soiled gloves and shove them deep in my back pocket. Closing my ZT, I pocket that next, then drop to the dirt. Burke was clutching his throat after I sliced it, blood slicking his palms, his fingers, the webs on his hands. After he dropped, he landed on his belly, arms folded beneath him.

I snag his left bicep, jerking his dead weight until I can see his bloody hand.

I'm not familiar with stiffs. I took a couple of anatomy classes when I started out at CSU after I got shipped across the country to the West Coast, but I was still grieving Heather then. I stuck it out two years before I gave up, swapping college out for trade school, where I learned how to be one hell of a mechanic.

Rigor mortis is a thing. I don't know how long it takes before it sets in, but now that Burke's dead, there's something he has that I want. I'll cut the damn thing off if I have to, but since he still has some warmth to him, I can save the damage to my knife by just tugging it off myself.

The blood on his fingers acts like the perfect lube for me to work Burke's wedding band off. I palm it once I have, barely noticing the red streaks covering my skin now that my gloves are gone.

I add the ring to my pocket, then rise up, kicking his outstretched hand away from me. My phone's in my car. Leaving Burke in the gravel where he belongs, I stride over to the open door, leaning in to grab my phone from its place in the console.

For all of my flaws and my... differences, I'm not a career criminal. I just have a unique perspective when it comes to learning, loving, and protecting my girls. Nothing is off-limits—and now I can add murder to the list—but the only time I've ever been in over my head like this, there was one person I could rely on.

And, lucky for me, my cousin *is* a career criminal.

Royce McIntyre is technically my cousin, but we've always been as close as brothers. Five years older than I am, he's the protector who's spent his whole life looking out for me. I'm the fuck-up who lets my dick and my obsessions get the better of me.

I've been good. Since Heather, I haven't felt that draw to another woman. That all-consuming need to possess and claim... I've been so fucking *good*. I had 'normal' relationships with a handful of girls in LA and even a few one-night stands that I had no problem walking away from the morning after.

Then I met Simone Burke, and I realized that I'd simply been waiting for her all along.

I didn't know what to do with her husband's corpse. Leaving it here would make it obvious he was murdered, and the last thing I want is for the keystone cops in Merrill Grove to think she has something to do with it.

Strong as I am, I can't lift Burke's deadweight and move him out of sight by myself unless I want my blood-speckled shirt to be blood-soaked. Leaving him sprawled out on his belly on the ground is a bad idea.

Cars rarely come down this way, but if they do, someone might see Burke before I can get rid of him.

I can't move this guy completely, even if I do grab his wrist and drag him further from where he fell. His car? With the keys still in the ignition, I start the engine, driving it so that the shiny Beemer is parked right on top of Burke. There. Maybe they'll see a car, but they won't see the victim.

After that, I head to my rented home to take a shower. I tried calling Royce, but he's been hard to reach lately. Distracted, and I don't blame him. Once I'm changed, I call him again and again until, about three hours after I killed Will Burke, my cousin answers, and I confess what I did to him.

As pissed as he was to hear I was in trouble again, Royce told me he'd be by as soon as he could to help me.

Springfield is an hour out of Merrill Grove. Knowing my cousin, he'll have to run his trip out of the city by his boss, but that shouldn't be a problem—and it isn't.

He gives me a twenty-minute warning, letting me know that he's almost to the small town. I tell him much better directions to the abandoned alley where I left Burke, then whistle as I leave through the front door, waving at my nosy neighbor across the way before sliding into my driver's seat.

Simone's driveway is still empty. That's not a surprise. She has a prized pink convertible that she keeps parked in her attached garage, and since I was full of shit when I told her husband she had a job, odds are that she's holed up in her house, hoping Burke doesn't come back.

Don't worry, baby. He *won't*.

PROLOGUE, PART II

JAKE

My instructions are top-notch, but I'm waiting next to Burke's car—and, well, *him*—for fifteen minutes before Royce rolls up in a discreet black car.

He's not alone, either.

I expected that. I might have called my cousin, but Royce is more than that. He has a specialized crew that does exactly what I needed help with, so of course he'd bring a couple of guys with him.

I've always blended in with a crowd. Royce? He got all the good McIntyre genes because his blond hair, blue eyes, and pretty face has him standing out wherever he goes. Even next to the doom-faced suits flanking him, he looks like an actor playing the part of mafia fixer instead of being one of the most powerful —and dangerous—men in Springfield.

The scowl that twists his handsome features when he sees I've been amusing myself, absently kicking Burke's scratched-up, bloody hand with the tip of my boot makes me doubt my earlier impression.

Whoops. I tried to play it off earlier that I was remorseful, that I didn't *mean* to kill Simone's husband, it just *happened*... but Royce knows me. He knows better.

After all the shit I've put him through, my poor cousin has probably been waiting for a call just like this one. I know him, too. He'd hoped that I'd give up on Simone once I realized that she was married to another man.

Maybe if she was happy, I would've. Maybe if she didn't glance at me outside of the convenience store, tears glittering against her pretty brown eyes, snaring my attention, obsession, and devotion in a fucking heartbeat... this might not have happened.

But it did, and though Royce's crew will make it so that no one has to know that it did, the stolen wedding ring in my pocket tells a different story, doesn't it?

Thinking of that, I smile, and Royce's scowl only deepens.

He nods at the car. "Is that what we have to get rid of?"

"The car and what's underneath it."

"Right." Glancing over his shoulder, he addresses the two other guys. "Killian. Bruno. Let's move the wheels and get the DB. I want him wrapped up and put in the trunk, then we can scrub the scene, dump the car, and get the hell back home in no time."

Royce turns back to me. "Keys, Jake?"

They're in my t-shirt pocket. I snag them, passing them to Royce. "Here you go."

He tosses the keys to Killian. "Get started. I gotta have a quick word with my cousin."

"You got it, Rolls." The dark-haired suit jerks his chin at the taller, bald-headed man with a flat expression. "C'mon Bruno. Grab the kit from our trunk and meet me by the BMW."

Bruno grunts, but does what he's told.

Royce nods in approval, then grabs me by my upper arm, muscling me a good fifteen feet away from his two guys.

I give him my most innocent grin. "Thanks for coming, Royce. I really appreciate it."

He huffs. "Cut the shit, Jake. Devil's got me keeping an eye on you, making sure you don't start any trouble on our turf, and what do you do? Slice up a man where I can't just drop everything to help you."

"I didn't *plan* this—"

He arches his eyebrows. I chuckle softly, knowing as well as him that I'm full of shit.

Hey. It was worth a try.

Royce runs his fingers through his perfectly-styled hair. "What were you thinking? Did you really believe you could just kill someone and not have any consequences from it?"

Why not? The Sinners do it all the time, and as their self-proclaimed clean-up man, no one knows that better than my cousin.

Royce is the second to the Devil of Springfield, the head of the Sinners Syndicate. As Devil's right-hand man, my cousin could have any job in their mafia, but his official title is 'underboss'. If you ask Royce, he's also a 'fixer' because he can do anything, get anything, arrange any goddamn thing with little more than his charm, his looks, his connections, and his name.

Ask me how I know. Considering we're both McIntyres, even if I'm the younger fuck-up, sharing the same name as my cousin is the only thing that saved my ass after I got in over my head with Heather Valiant.

He cleaned up my mess back then. Shipping me out of state, giving me the money to go to CSU, checking in with me over the years... Royce took care of me then. Driving out of Springfield with his crew in tow, ready to disappear Burke for me, he's still doing it.

I love him, but Royce is so damn predictable. He still harbors all this guilt for interfering in my relationship with Heather and how he was the one who was meeting with her the night she was killed by a member of Royce's rival gang. I didn't blame him, not even when he tried to tell me to move on before she betrayed me by turning to my cousin; if anything, I'm grateful he helped me see that Heather wasn't worthy of my love.

That's alright. Simone will be.

"He hurt her," I say, trying to explain my side in a way he'll understand. "That prick came after her. Don't tell me you wouldn't do the same for Nicolette—"

A muscle tics in his cheek as I mention the girlfriend he probably didn't think I knew about. Like, really? He kept his eyes on me, but Simone's not the only one I pay attention to, and now we both know it.

After a moment, Royce sighs. "Point taken. Fine. I'll handle the rest of the clean-up like I said I would. But this isn't Sinner territory, Jake. We're not on the West Side. You're playing with fire. It's going to burn you eventually."

I shrug. "He thought Simone was his."

"And now?"

She'll be *mine*, and that's all that matters.

Taking my silence as answer, Royce huffs again before turning to check on his crew. Bruno is taping the tarp around Burke's ankles while Killian is sprinkling some kind of powdery shit on the bloodstains. Looks like they're making good time of it, needing no help from my cousin at all.

He realizes it at the same time. So, instead of barking further orders at his guys, he decides to give me a little advice.

Leaning in, he squeezes my shoulder as he says,

"Listen. She's here. You're here. The husband's out of the picture now so it's up to you to make a move if that's what you want. A little tip? Be a nice guy. Get to know her. Maybe ask her out on a date, huh? Obsession isn't healthy. It isn't love, either."

That's rich, coming from Royce.

Since I already blew up my spot by mentioning Nicolette once, I might as well do it again. "Aren't you the one who sat outside your girlfriend's house for months, stalking her?"

The look he gives me tells me that an all-consuming need to be close to our girls is another McIntyre trait.

Royce bumps my shoulder with his palm. "Yeah, but then I got the chance to go on a date with her. Now we're together."

"Before or after you won a night with her in a bet?"

The bump becomes closer to a shove. "You got me all the way out here in bumfuck nowhere and you're gonna be an asshole? Don't be an asshole, Jake."

I'm not. I'm messing around with my older cousin because his helping me with Burke's body is a huge weight off my shoulders, but I'm not trying to be a dick or anything. Not to Royce. But he has his way of showing love and affection to the woman he's obsessed with, and I have mine.

Maybe... maybe it's time I give his a shot. After Casey, after Heather... if I hadn't intercepted Will Burke this morning, would I have lost Simone, too?

Third time's the charm, but I don't know anyone who's holding out hope for number *four*.

I want Simone.

I'll do anything to have her.

Even take advice from the man who nearly stole Heather away from me when my second love became obsessed with *him* instead.

I bat the front of Royce's suit jacket with the back of my hand. "I'll try. I won't make any promises, but I'll try."

After all, for the hope of forever with Simone Burke and the chance to make her a McIntyre, I'll do *anything*.

GOOD THING ROYCE GAVE ME ADVICE. BY THE TIME HE was hopping in his car, speeding out of the alley like a bat out of hell, I'm pretty sure my cousin isn't going to want to talk to me again anytime soon.

I don't blame him. If I got a phone call that something happened to Simone, that she was *missing*, the whole fucking world would be my collateral damage.

Because that's what happened. Just as we were waiting for the call that Killian and Bruno had gotten rid of the body and ditched the car, Royce's phone rang —but it wasn't Killian on the other end of the line. It was Lincoln Crewes, Devil himself, with the news that Royce's girlfriend up and disappeared.

She has ties to the Dragonflies, just like Heather did. Me and Royce... we were both thinking it. The Libellula Family treats their women like property, and if Nicolette had a run-in with one of them, it's no surprise that Royce would freak the fuck out like he did.

I've never seen my suave older cousin so out of control. He recovered quickly, though the same insane glint I see reflecting back at me in the mirror was flickering in Royce's eyes as he ended the call, then made a quick one to Killian.

Royce couldn't stick around to drive them back to Springfield. He needed to go *now*, and none of us were going to stop him.

I know my cousin. He carries a Beretta for protection, but I'm the only McIntyre who's ever killed a man.

Not saying that Royce isn't capable of murder. As the underboss in the Sinners Syndicate, he can end a life with a couple of words. But he's never pulled the trigger and killed a man himself.

Right now? I feel sorry for whoever took his girl. Who knows? We might both pop our 'murderer' cherries today.

I didn't want to be his first sacrifice because, blood or no blood, the way he snapped at me when he told me what Devil said... his trigger finger was itching, I'll tell you that much. I think the only thing that saved my ass was offering to drive out and pick Killian and

Bruno up at the meeting point myself, taking them back to Springfield once the clean-up of Will Burke's body was completely done.

He nodded, reining in his fury before sliding into the driver's seat of his car. Without another word, he peeled off, and I took one last look around the alley where I killed Burke before hopping in my own car.

By the time I'm pulling up to my driveway again, it's almost dark. I'm hungry, I'm exhausted, and I have a ten-hour shift tomorrow since I called Frank and asked for today off.

I'm still carrying Burke's ring in my pocket, and I need to do something about that. More importantly, as I back into the drive, positioning my car so I'm facing Simone's house, my tired body comes alive when I see the light bleeding through her bedroom window, a single silhouette on the shade as she moves around behind it.

My hand drops to my crotch. Watching her, starved for the sight of my sweet vixen, I make do with the silhouette, imagining what she must look like in there.

I could grab my phone. Pull up the camera I hid in her room, see exactly what she's doing... but there's something infinitely more erotic about watching her from just outside, fantasizing over her instead.

I scoot down in my seat, bracing my legs behind the steering wheel. Then, when I'm as comfortable as I can get, I slowly pull down the zipper on my jeans.

And with the same hand that slaughtered her husband only this morning, I stroke my cock leisurely as I watch *my* Simone, knowing that it'll only be a matter of time and a little more planning before there are two silhouettes on that shade...

PART TWO

OBSESSION

"I WILL HAVE YOU
YES, I WILL HAVE YOU
I WILL FIND A WAY
AND I WILL HAVE YOU
LIKE A BUTTERFLY
A WILD BUTTERFLY
I WILL COLLECT YOU
AND CAPTURE YOU…"

Obsession, Animotion (1983)

ONE
DEAD HUSBAND

SIMONE

My husband is dead.

I never saw a body, but that doesn't change the fact that I've been haunted by his ghost for months now. Ever since I received the envelope in my mailbox a couple of weeks after Will seemed to fall off the face of the Earth, I've known he was dead, that I was to blame, and whether he's a real ghost or I've fucking lost my mind, he won't leave me the hell alone.

He haunts my dreams. He stars in my nightmares. I see him everywhere, hear his voice in my head, and know that—even in death—he's holding me to the vows I was too naive to understand.

'Til death do us part... if only. He *has* to be dead, but he's here in my kitchen, hovering in the corner while I focus on my laptop screen, absently scrolling through Amazon, adding things to my cart.

He's wearing the same outfit he always is. The last time I saw Will, it was mid-March, and he had on a dark grey coat, black pants, and sneakers. It's May now, a pleasant spring morning in Merrill Grove, and I put all of my coats, jackets, and sweatshirts away in the spare bedroom a few weeks ago. The kitchen is especially warm, and if Will was still alive and really here, he'd be sweating under that coat.

Me? I'm sweating under his unblinking stare.

I can't escape him. I've known William Burke for eight years, ever since I met him my second year of college when I was nineteen. I'd completely reinvented myself out of high school, and I was so flattered when Will asked me out the first time. A well-known lacrosse player for Fairview University where we both attended, I thought he might be the one to make me feel loved. Safe. *Protected.*

That's all I wanted, and Will gave me all that and more—until we were married fresh on the heels of graduation and the mask slipped.

Once Simone Walton became Simone Burke, I got to know the real Will. The man who had certain ideas about how he expected his wife to act. Forget the fact that I got my BA in communications. Will's wife would stay at home while he went to the office every single week day. I'd cook for him, clean for him, fuck him whenever he wanted, and he'd provide for both of us. Easy enough even without his job since the Burkes always had more money than they know what to do with, but with his wealth came the arrogance he was careful to conceal during our dating years.

Married? I was trapped, looking for a way out until I thought I might've found one.

It didn't work. Not the way I hoped, at least, and all that happened was that Will left me with a black eye, bruises around my throat, and the resolve to get away from him before he actually killed me the next time. I did my research. I know the statistics. Once an abuser escalates to strangling, odds of him killing his partner increase exponentially.

I told him I wanted a divorce, and he strangled me. So I took off one night with nothing more than the clothes on my back, the ring on my finger, and as much cash as I could carry.

But online shopping proved to be my downfall, and when I used one of Will's cards to ship something to the house I'm renting here in Merrill Grove, he found me.

Will was only ever a monster behind closed doors. In the cul de sac I moved into, there's always someone watching. The night he found me, he stopped banging on my door when he realized he had an audience, promising he'd be back in the morning.

But he never returned—and that was all I needed to know even before I received the envelope.

Two weeks. For two weeks, I trembled behind my locked door, staring at my phone, waiting for it to ring. I blocked Will when I ran, but when he disappeared, I unblocked him, trying to see if he would answer just so I would *know*.

He never answered. I texted him, left voice messages, promised him things I had no intention of letting him have... but Will was gone, and with me the only living family he has, I don't think anyone gave a shit except for maybe his boss at work.

Two weeks... and then, on one of my rare trips to the mailbox, grabbing the junk mail so that my post office worker didn't think I'd died or something, I found a letter addressed simply to *Simone*.

No stamp on it. No return address; mine wasn't scrawled on it, either. Just my name and a solid lump tucked inside the sealed envelope.

I think I knew what it was even before my shaky fingers tore open the flap. Tipping the envelope over, my mind went blank as a dull gold band, dotted with brown, fell into my palm. I didn't need to see the inscription inside of it—the date we were married in Connecticut—to know it was Will's.

Just like I didn't need to know what dried-up,

flaking blood looked like to tell Will's wedding band was covered in the stuff.

There was a note, too. Part of me wanted to chuck it before reading it, but I never would have forgiven myself if I did. So, breathless and afraid, curious and determined, I pulled out the torn scrap of paper from the envelope and read it to myself:

And that's how I learned that, in the cul de sac, someone is always watching—and they're watching *me*.

The Watcher... I don't know who they are. The handwriting was careful, each letter printed exactly, capitalized and spaced perfectly. Only the signature seemed to have any personality; that, plus the message, made me convinced the Watcher is a man.

A man who got his hands on my dead husband's wedding ring...

Before I could think better of it, I put the bloody ring in a small plastic bag, then hid it in my pajama drawer. With those ominous words running through my mind—*consider yourself single... for now*—I took off mine, too.

That one went right into the trash where it belongs. So did the note... before I plucked it back out and hid that with the ring.

Did I call the cops? Fuck no. Instead, I waited a few more weeks on edge, and though I told myself at the time it was because I expected another note from the Watcher, the truth is that I spent all that time convinced the cops would come to me, telling me that Will was dead and that I was going down for his murder.

That never happened, and a month later, the only one accusing me of being responsible for his death is Will himself.

I know that's just my guilty conscience. Any time he hit me, I wished him dead. A dead Will couldn't hurt me—but he sure the hell can fuck with my mental state.

Just like he's doing right now.

Will is hazy. Because he's a ghost I've conjured up myself, he looks like one. If I stare at him head-on, I can see right through to the refrigerator behind him. He's in the same familiar pose—arms crossed over his chest, cheeks hollowed, legs crossed at the ankle—as he glares in that old familiar way at me.

I ignore him, adding a pair of fuzzy pink slippers to my cart.

"Another pair," my dead husband snorts. "Don't you have three already?"

In Springfield, I did. When you're fleeing from your abusive ex, snatching your bunny slippers from the closet is the last thing on your mind. I've been slowly but surely buying up the things I need to make me feel like I'm truly at home, and slippers seem pretty essential at this moment.

Or maybe I'm just getting a perverse sort of pleasure, spending all of Will's money while I can.

I know he's dead. No one else does. I'm sure his work noticed he stopped showing up, but Will was very particular. Every single one of our bills was withdrawn out of his account automatically. So long as the rent is paid and the utilities stay on, who needs to know that he's gone? And since he's not spending his money...

The slippers come in both light and dark pink. As a fuck you to the mental image of my late husband, I also add the second pair.

Will huffs. "Look at me, Simone. Not the damn screen. We need to talk about this."

"We don't need to talk about anything," I mutter under my breath.

"You *killed* me—"

"I didn't do it." It comes out in a singsong voice. I'm cracking up, I know it, and not even distracting myself with the promise of instant gratification and another slew of brown packages being dropped off on my front porch is helping. "It wasn't me."

"Just like Simone. It's never your fault, huh? It's always someone else."

It *was* someone else—and I think I know who, too. *The Watcher...*

"Shut up, Will." I never would've had the balls to say that to my husband while he was alive, but he's not, and he can't hurt me anymore.

He huffs again, definitely *not* shutting up. "Why? You know I'm telling the truth—"

"No. I know that you're not *real*," I snap back, and the fact that I have to means I need the reminder myself. "So just leave me the fuck alone."

I never had the nerve to tell Will to 'shut up' before, but how many times did I beg him to give me some space until I finally took some for myself? Too damn many, and he always refused to listen.

But I'm in control now.

Will vanishes in a wisp of nothingness, doing just what I commanded: leaving me all alone in the kitchen with only my laptop and a full shopping cart for company.

I rub my eyes, then squint, making sure he's really gone. Only when I assure myself that he is—for now, for now, *for now...*—do I return to the keyboard.

Know what? I think I need a fuzzy pink bathrobe to match my new slippers.

TWO
RUBY

order mostly everything I need online. It's habit. Will's definition of stay-at-home wife meant that I could rarely leave the apartment in Springfield. Only when it was something he needed instantly, or that couldn't be delivered, did he give me *permission* to go out on my own. More often than not, he expected me to wait until he got off of work so he could join me, my ever-present shadow, but on a few occasions, I was actually allowed out on my own.

I'm still getting used to doing that now. That if I want to run to the grocery store, Target, or grab something to eat without cooking it myself or waiting for delivery, I *can*. Merrill Grove isn't as big or populated as Springfield, but it's a cute little town where I thought I'd be safe.

And, thanks to an anonymous man known only as the Watcher, I think I am.

I don't know who he is. I'm only guessing when I think of him as a man, and maybe I'm making this all up in my head, too, because I haven't heard from him since he sent me Will's wedding ring. I still can't shake the feeling that I'm under a microscope, even when I look around and no one else is there—not even my dead husband.

But the message... the unsaid threat—or maybe promise—in the *for now* has me obsessing more and more over the Watcher lately. Is that why he targeted my husband? I thought it was because of me, but maybe not in the way I first believed.

Does he want to be my savior—or my next lover?

And why doesn't the idea that he killed Will to get to me scare me the way it should?

Because it totally should. I've never been brave; running is always my MO when I'm in trouble. And I've been in trouble more times than I can count in my life.

Shit. What is it about me that I've always seemed to attract the most broken, the most controlling, the most possessive partners? Will wasn't the first, though his unruly mop of hair and the dimple in his cheek were enough to hide his darker side until he had me locked down as his wife.

I don't know what kind of man—if he *is* a man—the Watcher is. A secret hero or a hidden villain, there's no way for me to, and since I've only heard from him once, I do my best to force myself to forget about him.

That goes about as well as me trying to banish the ghost of Will Burke. Since I had another nightmare about him last night, you can see exactly what I mean.

But I'll try. I have to. Will's gone, the Watcher is a mystery, and Simone has to do what Simone needs to to survive.

Today that means going to the local grocery store to stock up both my fridge and my pantry.

Paying to get my groceries delivered is the one service I don't use. I don't know why, but the idea of someone going around the store, picking out my food for me when I could do it myself bothers me. I don't doubt they'll be able to grab the right box of cereal, but I'm more particular when it comes to my fruit, veggies, and the type of ice cream I like. Soda, too. It has to be a certain flavor, specific brand, and I don't want to be that picky customer who complains when it's wrong.

Besides, it's probably a good idea to get out of my house every now and then. Especially since I can't shake the feeling that Will's haunting the inside and some faceless man is watching the outside, I need a few moments to myself when I can pretend that I haven't lost my mind.

Because I have. I can't deny that I have, but honestly? I lost my mind when I lost Will, and that seems like a fair trade-off to me.

Luckily, I'm a pretty decent actress when I need to

be, and whenever my next-door neighbor flags me down on the rare occasion I'm heading out to my car, you'd never know I'm tiptoeing along the thin line between batshit crazy and just a teensy bit insane.

I love my car. It's my most prized possession and has been for years. My fixation with it started back when I was a little girl. All I ever wanted was to get big and drive a pink convertible just like the Barbie dolls I played with. Why not? I mean, I had long blonde hair like Barbie did and a fondness for the color pink, and I swore I would one day have a convertible like hers.

Growing up, my family moved around a lot, thanks to my dad; it's mainly why I don't have a problem just up and leaving if I have to, even if I was rarely happy whenever we used to. I remember being a bitchy teen who made my parents' lives miserable the last time my dad's job had us moving a state over smack-dab in the middle of my high school career.

As a bribe, my parents promised to get me that pink convertible once I graduated if I would stop complaining about switching schools. With that dangling in front of me like a carrot on a stick? I shut the fuck up real quick.

My whole life, we were comfortable, but not rich; compared to the Burkes, we were probably on the lower end of middle class. Since I stubbornly insisted on a certain color and type of car, my options were limited. I ended up with a used 1999 Mazda Miata X5 in light pink with a convertible top that my parents handed me the keys to the day I received my diploma.

Eleven years later and I still baby the shit out of it. This car is basically my trademark, and when I was first hiding out from Will, I kept it in the garage so he wouldn't see it and know I was here. It's only been since the Watcher sent me that fateful note that I've felt comfortable enough leaving it in the driveway.

What can I say? I've always been a bit of a show-off.

The top's up today since the forecast called for rain earlier. But it's nice out now, and I'm thinking about lowering the top during the drive over to the store when I hear a familiar whistle, followed by a cheery voice calling out, "Good morning, Simone!"

It's not Will's judgy tone bouncing around my head. That's the only reason why I summon a small smile to my face as I turn to look over my shoulder, my ponytail nearly slapping me in the ear with the force of my quick swivel.

Damn it. I thought I snuck out of my house without anyone seeing me, but I momentarily forgot that, while the Watcher might be out there somewhere, he's not the only one...

It took me almost a year to get to know my neighbor in Springfield. Will and I lived in an apartment building, too, so you have to work to avoid someone living so close. He expected it, though, and it wasn't worth the argument to fight him on it.

In Merrill Grove, Ruby introduced herself to me

the first time I popped my head out of the house after I moved in. A woman about two decades older than me, with dyed dark hair, slight wrinkles surrounding her hazel eyes, and a nose the perfect length for her to keep sticking it into everyone's business, she's friendly. *Too* friendly, I think sometimes, but if there's one thing Ruby's going to do, it's chit chat with everyone in the cul de sac.

"Morning." I wave at her, making sure she sees my keys so that she knows I'm on my way out.

It's pointless. In my experience, that won't stop my neighbor. Since she's wearing her scrubs, it's obvious that she's heading for her shift at the hospital, but she still crosses the grass between our driveways so she doesn't have to call out to me again—and so that I can't climb into my car and escape her.

As usual, her eyes immediately dart to my left hand.

I swallow a sigh.

Ruby's never come out and asked me about it, but the first time she came over to introduce herself, I was still wearing my wedding ring. Add that to how she *did* ask me about the handsome man with the curly sand-colored hair who came to visit me, and I know she had to have been peeking out her window when Will found me two months ago. I can only imagine what conclusions she's come to about my love life, but at least she's been good enough to keep them to herself.

Oh, Simone. You should've known better than to think that would last...

"Where you off to? It's gorgeous out. Got a morning date?"

Right. Because she's seen enough of my comings and goings to know that I don't work or really leave the house that much at all. I doubt she actually thinks I'm going out to meet someone for breakfast, and when I shake my head and lightly tell her I'm going for groceries, my nosey neighbor makes it obvious that her first question was just the opening she needed for her *next* one.

"Oh, but you're single, though, aren't you, Simone?"

Not that it's any of her business, but... "Yup. It's just me, Ruby. I'm not hiding a boyfriend or anything in my house."

She laughs, taking it as the cheeky yet mild retort I intended for it to be.

Now, if she knew that it's not a living boyfriend I'm hiding, but how I'm being haunted by the vision of my dead husband? Yeah... she wouldn't be laughing then, would she?

My fake smile wavers. Ruby's laugh fades a little before she bolsters her own grin, patting my shoulder in a too-friendly gesture.

"I didn't think you were doing any such thing, hon. But, well, that's what has me popping over this morning. I've been thinking about tit... what's your take on the McIntyre boy?"

Boy? "I'm sorry. Who?"

She jerks her thumb over her shoulder toward a house about six down from mine. It's on the other side of the cul de sac, directly opposite of my place.

"Jake. He moved in a little after you did, taking over the Martins' rental through the summer. He came by yesterday to mow my yard for me since I had a double shift. Seems sweet. Might be a good match for you."

A boy who's mowing her lawn for her? "Um, thanks, Ruby, and I know I look kinda young"—*thank you, Dr. Pavil, for all the work I had done after my accident*—"but I'm going to be twenty-eight, so—"

Another laugh from Ruby, even heartier than the last. "No, no, no, Simone. Don't get the wrong idea. Jake's gotta be about your age. Twenty-six, twenty-seven... I don't know. When you hit fifty like I did last year, everyone under thirty starts looking like a kid to you."

Well, then. That makes me feel a little better about what she's suggesting before I realize just what she *is* suggesting.

Ruby Douglas, matchmaker, huh?

Consider yourself single... for now.

How would the mysterious Watcher like it if he knew my neighbor was trying to set me up with another guy?

A thrill runs through me that I quickly banish. I *am* single, and I'm pretty sure I've seen Jake around whenever I stood at my window, looking at the quiet neighborhood, wondering what kind of secrets are hidden behind the same white-painted doors...

I make a non-committal sound in the back of my throat. "Have a nice day at work, Ruby," I tell her, pressing the button on my key fob to unlock the doors, effectively ending the conversation.

She narrows her gaze for a moment, there and gone again, before she grins so widely, all I see are the apples of her cheeks. "Talk to you soon, hon. Yeah?"

Honestly? Not if I can help it.

I'M ABOUT TWO MILES DOWN THE ROAD WHEN I remember that I was going to lower the top of my car. It's nowhere near as busy in Merrill Grove as it is in Springfield, but I throw on my hazards anyway, then pull off to the side of the road.

Taking the top down on a Mazda requires parking the car and focusing on what I'm doing. It has handles on it that you grab after you release it from the anchor. That done, you help feed it toward the back of the car until it catches.

I've done it a million times. And every single time I have, the power windows go down, either on their own or with another help. Sometimes I have to open the door to get the mechanism working, but as I'm trying to take the top down now, the windows don't budge.

Not even when I open the door or try killing the engine, then restarting the car.

That's weird.

I fiddle with it a few minutes more, growing more and more anxious when I can't get it to work. This car is so special to me. I've treated it well since I've had it, barely putting that many miles on it since Will didn't like me driving around on my own, but I've routinely gotten it serviced, starting it up frequently and taking a spin around the block even when I knew I'd get a lecture from my husband for doing so.

It's in pristine condition for one main reason: whenever something goes wrong, I don't try to figure it out myself. Will knew fuck-all about cars, and no matter what it cost me to make him happy, I got the money from him to bring my baby to the garage whenever I needed to.

Now? I don't need to beg my husband for any funds. I have a debit card with my married name on it that's linked straight to his account—and no selfish prick to tell me off for using it.

Groceries can wait. I need to get my car looked at.

And, thank fucking God, there's a garage nearby that I've passed every time I've gone this way to get to the grocery store.

THREE

ABOUT TIME

JAKE

My nerves are fucking shot.

It's been four days since I decided that I've done enough watching. I've done enough research. At this point, I think I know Simone better than even *she* does, and I'm ready to move ahead with the next step of my plan.

Like I said. I'm a planner. I've learned to be since my past reckless behavior has only ever lost me my girls in the past.

First, there was Casey. Casey Mead. My first love, and the one I thought I would be with forever.

I still remember the day she walked into Mr. Madison's eleventh grade history class. She had her pretty blonde hair falling like a sheet down her back, her soft brown gaze cast down on the floor, hugging her books to her chest as Mr. Madison told her to take any free seat.

Scott Genovese whistled at her, then tapped the back of the empty seat in front of him. Casey got the look of a startled deer on her face, frozen in place at the front of the room, eyes darting from Scott's smug grin to any available desks nearby.

Then she saw me. Average build. Average height. Plain brown eyes, plain brown hair, and an expression that said she could trust me. I wouldn't bother her. She'd be safe.

Casey scurried over and plopped herself in the seat next to me, and from that moment on? She was *mine*.

But it didn't last. She was the one, but after spending junior and senior years together, she vanished after graduation. I wasn't as good at tracking down my girls then as I am now, and Casey seemed to simply disappear. I still search for her on social media —and obituaries—from time to time since I never really forget one of my girls, even when I have a new one. Nothing. When I was eighteen, she was gone, and I had to force myself to get over her.

I did with Heather Valiant.

Unlike my relationship with Casey, we weren't together *together*. It never got to that point. I was still watching her, stalking her, trying to get her to notice me—to *want* me—when Heather decided my obsession with her was too intense.

I was barely twenty. She'd just turned twenty-one,

the coddled younger sister of a member of the Libellula Family. I scared her, but she didn't go to the Dragonflies for help.

Nope. Heather went to the Sinners. Knowing Royce was my cousin, she went to him to see if he could get me to back off. She didn't realize how much danger she was putting him into by crossing over from the East End of Springfield to the West Side. Not from me; hurt as I was that Heather fell for Royce McIntyre instead of Jake, I do have *some* boundaries, and as long as Royce didn't betray me, I'd never blame my cousin for something he couldn't control. The Dragonflies, however, didn't like the idea of their property spreading their legs for a Sinner.

Royce never fucked Heather. I never got the chance to, either. As much as I loved her and would've given her the world, she got killed in the crossfire when a Dragonfly aimed for Royce and hit Heather instead.

And then she was gone.

To keep me from being collateral damage in the brewing turf war between the two mafias, Royce helped my parents ship me off to California. There were so many blondes there, I thought I'd be in trouble, but I didn't feel that spark again until I came home to visit for Christmas.

Simone...

I refused to make the same mistakes with Simone, especially since her marriage was a complication that made my feelings for her a little bit more challenging.

So I plotted. I planned. Even before she threw a curve ball at me, running from Will Burke, I was slowly but surely working my way into her life. I'd even put my name on the waiting list for her apartment complex after I completely shut down my life back in LA.

I had to. Simone was in Springfield which meant *I* had to stay in Springfield. Just like how she moved to Merrill Grove and now that's where I'll be.

At least it was a whole hell of a lot easier to find a house to rent near Simone in the small town. Luck was on my side, with one of the rentals willing to sublet a house on a month-to-month basis. I'm right here, and she has no idea.

Maybe I showed my hand a little early, sending her that note. I had to, though. Every time I caught a glimpse of Simone still wearing Burke's ring on her finger... it made me want to ask Royce where his crew buried the prick just so I could dig him up and stab him a couple of more times. Besides, she needed to know that she didn't have to look out her window, afraid she'd find Will standing there again. She was safe, and soon she'd be mine.

I won't lose her. Not this one. So, following Royce's advice, I didn't overwhelm her with my affection. Be the nice guy, he said. Considering he eloped with Nicolette last month, getting married in Las Vegas, maybe he's on to something. He has his girl.

I'll do anything for mine.

So I've been nice. I've watched her from the shadows, slipping into the trees across from her window, standing on the edge of my rented property so that I don't miss anything. I've done my research on her. Casey might not have any social media presence, but Simone has a few different profiles.

I obsess over them constantly, saving any photo she posts to my phone so that I have something to jerk off to while waiting until I can have the real thing. I take any post as gospel, making sure I know any and everything about my sweet vixen.

My impression of her hasn't changed. Like me, she presents an innocent appearance to the rest of the world, but there's something broken inside of her that calls to me. I'll fix her. I'll make her whole. Whatever it takes.

That was the initial stage of my plan. First, I needed to learn what makes Simone tick.

Next? I needed to infiltrate her life.

I've done that already. I'm that somewhat familiar, kind of forgettable face that you see around town and think, *do I know him*? We haven't been introduced yet—though not for a lack of trying. Simone rarely leaves her house, and even when I mowed her next-door neighbor's lawn for her the other day, trying to size up the chatty nurse to see if she knew anything about Simone that I didn't, I didn't get a single peek of her through the window.

I did, however, plant a seed in the woman's mind

that I'd be the perfect guy for the lonely new blonde who moved into the cul de sac...

That wasn't enough for me. I'll take it because it was an opportunity and I'll never let one pass me by, but already I've been thinking about how to get Simone to notice me without breaking into her house and introducing myself as the Watcher.

Not that I have any issue with doing that. Hell, I broke into Simone's house the first night I saw her leave it. Being a mechanic, I'm good with my hands. Even better with burglar tools. I slipped in through the back door where no one would see me, then spent twenty glorious minutes basking in being surrounded by everything *Simone*.

I stole a pair of silky panties before I left, leaving a pale pink rose on top of her dresser as a sign that I was there.

It was gone the next time I had the chance to sneak into her room, putting up another couple of cameras so that I could keep an eye on her when it was too risky to stand in the shadows across the street from her window. So I left another rose and watched her look at it in puzzled confusion before dropping it into her pajama drawer.

She doesn't seem to know they're from me. Maybe, next time, I'll leave her another note.

She kept my first note, too. I take heart in that, just like I did when I found Simone's wedding ring in the same drawer. It seemed like she got my message just fine: she's single now. Widowed. Whatever. Will Burke won't stand in our way any longer, and the sooner she accepted that, the better.

I wish that was done so easily. Considering I've caught her on camera, staring into the corner of her room, her kitchen, the living room, having a one-sided conversation with who could only be her dead husband... she doesn't seem to be grieving. Not like I did when Heather died. This is something else entirely, and there isn't anything I wouldn't do to help her get through this.

Except bring that fucker back to life.

No. She's better off without him. I'm the better man for her, and I'll just keep following the plan until she accepts *that*.

I need her to get to know *me*. Jake. What better way to get her to fall in love with me than by making myself available to her?

But how?

The answer came down to her car. While I've convinced myself that Simone never really loved Will Burke—not the way that I'll insist she love *me*—that pink car she kept in her garage is the true love of her life. It has to be. Bringing a car like that to a town like Merrill Grove... if she was trying to stay under the radar, that went out the fucking window as soon as she drove into town in a pale pink convertible, the wind catching her pretty, pretty blonde hair.

To get to Simone, my best bet was to go through her car. And, lucky me, I'm a mechanic.

I wouldn't destroy the Mazda. To do that would be to hurt Simone, but I could screw with the fuses, fuck with the window mechanism, and eventually she'd need to get it looked at.

Merrill Grove is small enough that there are only two garages on this side of town: Frank's and one called Tire Central. I charmed my way into a job at Frank's because it was closer to the cul de sac. Assuming she'd need to get her car serviced, knowing Simone as I do, she'd go there.

Only one problem: she wouldn't need to bring the car down to the shop until she got in for a drive and realized something was wrong.

It's been four days since I tampered with her car. I have a ten-day stint, working overtime to cover for Frank since he took his wife out on a cruise. Simone might not go out everyday, but I knew she'd go for a ride some time during the next week and half.

Four days into it, and I'm going stir-crazy, wondering why the fuck she hasn't yet.

And then, when it's just me and Brendon working on replacing a transmission for one of Frank's buddies in between oil changes and tire rotations for some of our other regulars, I catch a flash of pink out of the corner of my eye, and my cock immediately starts to harden.

The color does it to me. When it reminds me so

much of Simone, I've gotten sprung by just the shade of it. Same thing happens when I stop over at the local flower shop to pick up a few pink roses that I keep in case I want to leave one for Simone. Half the time I'm adjusting my hard-on while one of the clerks wraps them up for my 'wife'.

It was easier in Springfield. There's a shop there—Louise's, I think—where I used to buy flowers for Heather first, then sending them anonymously to Simone's apartment. She was this old married woman, running the shop, who suggested the pink roses to me in the first place. In Merrill Grove, the clerks are all girls around my age who seem to think they're special enough to get me to buy them flowers instead.

Even after I emphasized that these were for my wife—because Simone will be my wife one day—the two clerks smirked at each other before the brunette slipped a scrap of paper with her number on it into my bouquet.

As if my erection was for either of them. Fuck no. From the moment I decided Simone would be mine, it's my hand or nothing. The next time I sink my cock into a woman, it'll be her and only her—and she'll be the *last* one who ever gets it.

Because I'm not losing her. Not this woman. Not this time.

And I promise myself that again as Simone parks her car, then walks hesitantly up to the open garage where we're working.

I'm elbows-deep in this transmission right now. I wish I was fast enough to get my head out of the hood, but Brendon's already sizing Simone up by the time I'm standing, wiping my hands on one of the grease rags.

I catch the tail-end of their conversation as Simone's sweet voice asks, "Will that take long?"

Brendon smiles down at her. Simone is only a few inches shorter than I am, but Brendon seems like a fucking goofy ass giraffe next to her. He brags that he's six-five, though I'd put it him at six-two at the most, and seems to think his height will make up for any of his flaws.

Dickhead. He doesn't even notice that Simone is shrinking away from him.

Her bastard husband was about six feet tall. I can't imagine she feels comfortable standing next to a man even taller than that, especially when he's purposely using his height advantage to get a peek down her low-cut pink t-shirt.

His straw-colored hair is thick and straight, reaching his ears. He runs his fingers through the strands, then smirks. "Some guys might take all day for a fix like that. Not us. Give me a half an hour, hour tops, and I'll send you on your way, pretty lady."

Simone's smile freezes on her face, and I tell myself that Brendon deserves everything coming his way for spooking my sweet vixen.

Tossing the grease rag back onto the pile, doing my best not to stare at Simone, I say, "Hey, Bren. I'm gonna go grab a Coke from the vending machine. You want anything?"

He doesn't even bother to take his eyes off of her to answer me. "That's okay, Jakey. I got iced tea in the back."

I know that. Nice to have confirmation, though.

It takes every ounce of self-control I have to walk away as Brendon gets Simone sorted. He'll give her a clipboard to take down all of her info—since Frank's is an old-fashioned shop, and our cantankerous boss thinks computers are the devil—and tell her to sit down tight while we get right on her vehicle.

He's so fucking full of it. I know what's wrong with her car. I *did* it. It's a five-minute job at the most, maybe ten because he'll have to check it over first. But if Brendon is interested in a customer, he'll make them stick around longer, doing a little small talk as he acts like he's fixing their car.

I've seen him do it. Then, when he charges a small amount for the fix as a 'favor'—and not because most jobs are quick fixes that he draws out on purpose—the customer is so grateful for the discount, they're a whole lot more interested in him when he suggests they meet up for dinner—or sex.

And he thinks he's going to do that to *my* Simone?

FOUR

MAG CITRATE AND CONDITIONER

JAKE

On the pretense that I need to grab my wallet from the back, I take a quick detour to Frank's office.

The old man is overweight and pushing sixty. He had a colonoscopy my first week on the job, and though I learned just how much I'd rather drive home to shit than use the employee bathroom after that, I've been in here enough times to remember seeing the barely-drank bottle of liquid magnesium citrate he never had the chance to finish during his prep.

I snatch it, then head to the employee fridge. Brendon's iced tea jug takes up most of the space. Quickly unscrewing the cap to the jug first, the magnesium citrate next, I dump the entire contents of the bottle into it before tossing the empty into the recycling bin.

That done, I grab two bucks from my wallet, then head back out to the vending machine.

Brendon is making a big to-do of doing the diagnostics for Simone's car. I feel a sense of twisted righteousness at what I just did as I search for Simone.

She's studiously ignoring Brendon.

Good.

Striding over to the vending machine, I feed the first dollar into it.

With Simone sitting on the edge of one of our plastic chairs, watching the crooked television in the reception area, she can't see what I'm doing. I quickly jab the ginger ale button—

"Crap."

Brendon pokes his head out of the Mazda. "Something wrong, Jakey?"

"Vending machine spit this out instead of my Coke."

"Ah. That's shit luck."

I shrug. "It's fine. I got another buck. I'll try again. But you've got your iced tea..." I pause as though something just came to me. Crossing the garage, heading over to the reception area, I don't stop until I'm standing about three feet away from Simone.

Unlike Brendon, I'm not trying to spook her. I clear my throat, waiting for her to notice me.

When she does, I suck in a tiny breath, waiting to see if she'll recognize me. Either from all the times I got close to her in Springfield, or just from how long I spend outside in the cul de sac, giving her the chance to watch me, get used to me, before I slip into the shadows, watching her.

Damn it. Not a spark of recognition as she glances up at me questioningly.

That's fine. It's all going according to plan. She doesn't know me now—but she will.

I give her a grin. "Hey. Thirsty? I got a ginger ale I'm not gonna drink."

Her beautiful brown eyes light up. "Um. Yeah. I mean, if you're sure—"

I hold it out to Simone. "Take it. On the house."

See, Bren? I can hand out freebies, too. And, sure, I'm doing all of this according to the plan that will end with Simone in my bed, but it won't be a one-time thing. Let Bren get his casual sex somewhere else.

This one belongs to me.

Her nails are a pretty pink color, almost the exact shade as her car. She takes the can from me, opening it carefully so that she doesn't snap a fingernail. It fizzes and pops, and she smiles as she takes a small sip.

My cock twitches, aching to think about what it'll be like to have those lips wrapped around me.

A hint of my lust for her must slip into my pleasant expression because, suddenly, the heights of her cheeks turn pink.

Fuck. Why don't I just come in my pants while I'm at it?

"Thanks," she says, never once dipping her gaze from mine. "It's my favorite."

Oh, Simone...

I know that, too.

I END UP FINISHING THE TRANS JOB ON MY OWN.

Probably for the best. A transmission swap isn't all that difficult, but it takes a steady hand, an eye for detail, and a mechanic who knows what the fuck he's doing.

Brendon's a pretty decent mechanic when he's not thinking with his dick. He doesn't keep Simone waiting too long—I only get to watch her out of the corner of my eye for about forty minutes before he announces he's done—though I'm pretty fucking glad I doctored his iced tea when he suggests the two of them meeting up for dinner or drinks after the garage closes up.

He can *try*. Considering he spent nearly the whole rest of our shift in the bathroom, I'm thinking that's not gonna happen.

Every time he curses under his breath, then bolts for the back, I have to swallow my grin. Finally, when he starts walking funny on his way out to the garage, I can't keep myself from commenting.

"What's up with you? You okay?"

"Dunno. I've been shitting my brains out since lunch. I had tuna. You think it was bad?"

Maybe. Or maybe he's been guzzling his iced tea all afternoon, getting more and more laxative with every sip.

"Could be."

"Fuck. My ass is burning. I can't wait to get home and take a nice cold shower."

I fake a look of concern. "Home? But I thought you had a hot date tonight."

He thought so, too. Even though Simone gave him a non-committal answer, saying something about having to go shopping still, I know Brendon. If he got the hots for her, he'd be like flies on shit. He won't leave her alone.

Not unless I make him—and a nice round of explosive diarrhea should do the trick.

"Yeah. She was pretty hot. Nice tits. I told her that one of her hoses was looking questionable as a way to get her to come back sooner. Maybe I'll give her a shot next time."

Reminder, Jake: grab some more liquid mag citrate, just in case.

But because I've assured myself that Brendon won't be bothering Simone tonight, I feel magnanimous enough to let him head out early. I close up the garage myself at six, stop for dinner, then head home.

Simone's driveway is empty.

I don't even bother getting out of my car before I'm checking my phone, pulling up the app for the tracker I have on hers.

Even after two and a half months in this town, I'm not all that familiar with every part of it. I don't know at first glance where her car's parked, but once I zoom in, I see that she's at a local shopping mall.

A quick look-up reveals that their hours are ten to nine. It's only seven now. If Simone's gone shopping, looking for some retail therapy, she won't leave that mall until it closes.

I'm not worried that Brendon somehow got her to agree to go out with him. Even if he took her number off her paperwork, I put enough of Frank's magnesium citrate in Brendon's jug of iced tea to keep him confined to his house.

But Simone's? It's empty right now.

I smile. Not for long.

IT SHOULDN'T BE THIS EASY TO BREAK INTO HER HOUSE.

When I live with Simone, I'm going to install the best security system money can buy to keep my wife safe. Since doing that now would only make it more difficult for me to visit her while she's sleeping—or immerse myself in her space while she's out of it—I rely on my cameras to make sure no one else is slipping inside other than me.

I pull on my black mask as a precaution. My routine checks of her house tell me that it didn't come with a doorbell camera. She never installed one herself, either, though she might have if her bastard of a husband kept coming around. I'm glad she didn't because then I would've had to find a way around it instead of just changing from my coveralls to black jeans and a matching shirt, grabbing my mask, and yanking it on right before I let myself in through the back.

Our cul de sac is surrounded by a thick wooded area. It's shaped like a 'U', with my house and Simone's on opposite sides, and the woods bracketed the entire neighborhood. Moving soundlessly through the trees, following the same path I have for months now, I can go from my place to hers and never get caught.

I have this animalistic need to mark my territory, even if she has no idea that I'm here. Leaving her flowers is one way to do that, but since she acts as though they miraculously appear with no other ulterior motive, it doesn't satisfy my urge to catch her attention.

Writing her a note, signing it with an anonymous nickname... that helped. Even if she doesn't know who Jake is, I want her to obsess over the Watcher—and she does. I've lost track of how many times she's pulled out the note I sent with Burke's ring, running her fingers over the print, murmuring something to herself.

Of course, her face would change, and the murmur would turn into a louder mutter as she snaps something at a man only she can see. Will Burke is haunting my sweet vixen, and if she's anything like me, it's the lack of closure that's fucking with her.

She knows he's dead. I made it as obvious as I could without writing her another note that says: Yup, I did it. In time, I'll confess to her. I'll tell her everything, the good and the bad, just so she knows as much about me as I do her.

I won't be satisfied until she's as devoted to me, and when I know I have her love and affection and every goddamn emotion I can steal from her, I'll explain to her how I killed Burke, and just why he had to die.

And that's if she doesn't already suspect the truth...

Tonight, there's no sign of the ghost of Will Burke. It's quiet in here, the only sound coming from the wall clock in her kitchen. It's shaped like a lemon, a bit of whimsy in the otherwise empty space. There's a cheap table she picked up online, the wall clock, and a set of matching dishcloths, and that's about it.

I like the clock. The towels, too. They suggest to me that Simone plans on making this her home. Of maybe sticking around for a while instead of running away again.

The rest of her house is decorated the same way. A few stock pieces of furniture that would've been here when she rented the place with a handful of ornaments, pictures, and decorations that show off her personality.

In her upstairs bathroom, she has a frosted shower curtain, a pink toilet cover, matching pink rug, and a pair of towels that are, you guessed it, pink. It has a hint of sweetness lingering in the small room. Her body wash, or maybe the perfume she splashes on before she leaves the house. I'm not sure yet, and like I do when I have time, I pick up random bottles I find scattered about, opening the lids and breathing in deep.

I haven't gotten close enough to Simone to learn her true scent, the smell that is inherently *Simone*. I've caught whiffs of it, and it makes me rock fucking hard each time, but it's some kind of combination of all of these products that creates it.

There are so many. I've watched her through the camera I taped to the bottom of her mirror; the size of a Scrabble tile, I painted it white so it blends in with the wall behind it. I've lost hours of my life to studying her morning and evening routines, cataloging that in my file of everything Simone.

I recognize the bottles, though I need to do more research to learn what each of them does. If they help make my Simone's skin that dewy, her eyes beautifully bright, and her lips fuckably soft, I'll throw money at the companies so that she'll never run out if it makes her happy, even if I know fuck-all about any of them.

But there's one thing I'm pretty sure everyone uses when they take a shower, and after I put her bottles back where I found them, I tug the shower curtain back and grab her conditioner.

The first time I did this, I used her shampoo

because I'm a guy and I only wash my hair with shampoo. I thought about it after I slipped out of her house. She has long, beautiful hair. I might not use conditioner, but Simone probably does. The way my camera is angled, I can see the bathroom but not inside of the shower itself. It's a tub/shower combo, and the edge of it is in the picture, but with the curtain drawn, it's useless.

So I waited until I could go back and check. Of course she has conditioner. And that means she rinses out the shampoo, replacing it with the creamy stuff.

Oh, no, no, no. I want the last thing that touched her hair to have me in it. I don't care that she probably rinses that out, too. They make leave-ins, don't they? That's a thing. Right? If not, that's fine. The conditioner works until I can fill her pussy with all I have.

And that's why I've grabbed the conditioner every time I've snuck in here.

I'm fast. Not because I'm worried that Simone will return home and find me in here, but because I've been hard on and off since she walked into the garage earlier today. With Brendon stinking up the toilet, I couldn't rub one out real quick at work, so I suffered with blue balls while I finished up the car I was working on.

I finally went down after hours of agony, but that fucker came back to life the instant I walked into Simone's house. I'm so desperate for her, there's already a little pre-come beading at the tip of my poor erection when I yank down my jeans, releasing my cock from my boxers.

Closing my eyes, I imagine those pretty pink fingernails scraping the veins of my cock before her soft palm wraps around me. My own hands are callused as fuck, covered in grime until I can go home and scrub them off like I do nightly, but in my fantasy, it's *Simone* who starts stroking me off.

I grit my teeth, bracing my boots against the tile of her bathroom floor. The friction is painful which is only right. I don't deserve pleasure until I can convince Simone to be mine, and the way I'm rubbing my cock raw right now is all the motivation I need to work toward my ultimate prize.

The *one*.

My sweet vixen...

The memory of Simone's shy smile flashing before me has my sac tightening. I squeeze, tugging now, panting her name softly—*Simone, Simone, fuck me, Simone*—as I start to orgasm.

I'm ready. I opened the conditioner bottle before I began, and as soon as I start spurting, I grab it, angling the bottle to catch as much of my come as I can. Considering how many times I've jerked off into Simone's hair care products, determined to have my sweet vixen walk around with a little bit of me on her, you'd think I'd be better at this.

You'd be wrong.

I spill fucking *everywhere*. My hand, the sides of the

plastic bottle, around the rim, on her rug… I'm not pissed about that, though she might be if she had any idea. Way I see it, that's just another way to mark my territory, and I'm feeling a sense of pride as I use my finger to scoop up whatever I can before dabbing it inside the conditioner bottle.

Only once I'm satisfied that I got as much as I could in there do I re-cap it, then give the conditioner a good shake before putting it back where it belongs. That done, I tuck my cock into my boxers and pull my jeans back up. Leaving the button undone, I tug my flannel down as I use the tip of my boot to rub in the last of the jizz I couldn't gather up.

There. Simone might not know who I am just yet, but at least I marked her the only way I can.

For now.

FIVE
GUARANTEE

Call me paranoid, but even if I'm not planning on leaving the house, I get out and check on my car every morning and every night to assure myself that the windows are working right.

I've done that the last week and a half, ever since I brought it home from the garage. I keep expecting my poor baby to fail on me now after more than a decade of service, only breathing out a sigh of relief whenever I start the car, reach for the power window, and it eases down again.

After that, I go back inside. I can't help myself. Maybe I feel jinxed, like pushing my car too far will only end with me sitting in that run-down mechanic shop again, sipping on a ginger ale while watching Judge Judy. That's partly true, I gotta admit, but mostly it's this strange sense I've been getting lately that, whenever I *do* leave my house, someone takes advantage of my absence to let themselves in.

I don't have any proof. Proof? When you're an anxious wreck like me, having conversations with a figment of your imagination, you don't expect something as solid as *proof*. I think that's why I keep pulling the note from the Watcher out, reading it again and again if only because it is something tangible I can hold.

There's someone out there watching me. They know enough about me to be sure that Will Burke was my husband in order to send me his bloody wedding ring. Even if I have no idea how this mysterious figure got their hands on that ring—though all signs point to the really fucking obvious—there's no denying that this message was sent specifically for me.

For Simone.

I'm trying to move on from that. Just like how I've been going out more than I have, returning to in-person shopping if only because it gets me out of the house—and because part of me is still defiant enough... and maybe even still a bit too frightened—to stay where I know the Watcher can find me easily.

He wants to watch? Good luck. You gotta know where I am first...

Today I planned on sticking around the house. During my latest manic shopping binge, I got it in my head that I should paint the living room of my house. I e-mailed the landlord to see if I was allowed to, and I got a response back last night that said I could so long as I pay to have it repainted in the event of me moving out.

I don't see that happening anytime soon. I like Merrill Grove. It reminds me of Baker, the small town a state over where I grew up during my formative years before my dad started bouncing our family around like we were a bunch of ping-pong balls. When I first fled from Will, I almost wanted to return there. Only knowing that it would be the first place he searched kept me from going home; instead, I picked a town close enough like it that he'd never expect me to hide out in.

Of course, he found me anyway. And since he still won't leave me the fuck alone even after he died, there's no point in running anymore. He's stuck in my brain, after all. No matter where his body is now, if I leave Merrill Grove, he'll chase and he'll chase and he'll chase.

I've gotten used to the apparition following me around my house, bitching at me constantly like the real Will often did. It's so incredibly insane that it's kind of become commonplace. If it keeps up, I might have to go back to therapy like I did when I was a troubled kid, though how the hell do I explain that I'm seeing the ghost of my husband when no one else but me and the Watcher know for sure that he's gone?

No. If I ignore him, he'll eventually disappear. If I

find happiness... if I finally get the damn happily-ever-after I was promised so many years ago... he might get the hint and realize that this was all his fault.

It's possible, though I have to admit it's far more likely that I won't get his nagging voice out of my head until I get closure about how he died.

Why he died.

And if it's all *my* fault...

He's not real. He's *not*. I'm seeing him, but that doesn't make him *real*. He's in my house. He rides next to me in my car.

He watches me from outside the house, making me insane with the idea that I might never escape him, not even in death.

'Til death do you part...

Too bad my dead husband didn't get the memo.

On the plus side, he's been eerily quiet the last few days. I only thought I saw him out of the corner of my eye once or twice, then when I stood in front of my bedroom window, peeking up at the moon, staring out into the quiet cul de sac. I swore Will was taunting me from across the street, but when I lifted the window itself to poke my head out, getting a better look, there was nothing there.

There never is.

I'm not worried about my mind conjuring him now. It's bright out, the sun is shining, and the air is filled with the scent of flowers filtering to me from the Douglas's front garden. It's chaotic and unruly, but there's a method to the way the flowers—reds and yellows, whites and oranges—have been laid out.

I like it. I told Ruby that recently when she caught me inching closer to it, peering at all of the spring blooms.

She thought I was admiring her garden, and I was... but that's not all I was doing—

"Didn't I tell you we have a guarantee?"

So lost in what I was thinking about—as usual—I didn't even realize that someone had approached me until a familiar male voice rips me out of my reverie.

My head snaps up, fingers instantly curving around my key fob in case I need to use the key itself as a weapon. As soon as I see who's behind me, I relax my fingers a fraction.

It's a guy, obviously. A couple of inches taller than my five-five, he has a broad if stocky build that could either be sculpted muscle or solid fat; I can't tell because he's wearing a full set of dark grey coveralls despite it already pushing seventy degrees this morning. He has his brown hair cut short and slicked back. His eyes are a little darker, though there's a friendliness to them that puts me immediately at ease.

I focus on his face. At first glance, it seems almost boyishly handsome. Soft cheeks and thin pink lips. There's a hard edge to his jaw, though, and a hint of a dare to the smile he's giving me as he strides confidently up my driveway.

He's cute. Almost handsome, but definitely someone I could see myself becoming attracted to.

He's also familiar in a way that sings to me, and it takes me a moment to remember where I've seen him lately—and why it makes sense that he would be teasingly talking about a guarantee after he clearly caught me checking out my car again.

"I know you. You gave me the ginger ale while I was waiting for my car to be looked at."

His smile says he's pleased that I recognize him. "That's right. And all of our jobs down at Frank's come with a guarantee. If it breaks again because of our work, we'll fix it for free. Since Frank hates it when we screw up, he makes sure we do the job right the first time. Your window should be fine."

My window should be, but—

"Okay. That's fair. But what if one of your mechanics fixes one thing, then breaks another so that he can get me back in the shop to hit on me again?"

Holy shit. Where did that come from?

I'm not wrong. I've been thinking about that every time I come out here. I might play a little oblivious, but I can tell when a guy's into me. That doesn't stop me from falling for the wrong kind of man. I've done it a bunch of times, with Will only being the last one. I want to think I've learned from my mistakes, though, and if I'm going to get involved with a mechanic, it's not going to be the one who spent the entire time I was hanging around the shop trying to loom over me so he could stare down at my boobs.

However, there's my real-life lived experience as a woman, and then there's me blurting that suspicion out in front of one of his co-workers.

Who, with an amused look flashing in his eyes, doesn't seem to mind at all.

"Brendon's a little obvious, but he's a good guy." When I raise my eyebrows at him, he chuckles. "Okay. How about a professional? He won't fuck with a customer's vehicle because that would be fucking with Frank. I'm new in town. Even I know you don't fuck with Frank. Don't worry about Brendon."

"That's the guy who did my car, right?"

He nods.

"And who tried to ask me out to dinner because he did such a good job and only charged me for parts, not labor?"

He winces.

Exactly.

When you've been as obsessed with keeping your baby in as good of shape as possible as I have, you spend a lot of time at either the dealer or a garage. The guys there see a pretty blonde and think she knows shit about her car, and maybe I can't fix it myself, but that doesn't mean I'll let them pull that kind of stunt with me.

And now this guy knows it.

He lifts his hand, ruffling the back of his hair. "Would dinner with one of us have been so bad?"

"You his wingman?" I tease, turning his question into one of my own. That was a little flirty-ish to me, and suddenly I'm not so sure we're talking about his buddy anymore. "You're as bad as Ruby."

His eyes flicker over to my neighbor's house. "Ruby. Yes. I know Ruby."

There's something in the way he says that. I take a moment, running our short conversation through my head, then remember something else he just told me.

"Wait. You said you're new in town? Oh. Duh." I gesture at his coveralls—and the name *Jake* embroidered in script. "You're Jake."

His eyes light up in surprise before he lets out another chuckle. "You've heard of me?"

I shrug. "Like I said. Ruby."

"Well, that's me sorted. But what about you?"

Oh. I just assumed he knew.

I hold out my hand. "Simone."

He takes it. His hand is warm, yet a little rough, and I figure that has to do with his line of work. His nails are immaculate, though, and I like that.

"Nice to meet you, Simone."

"You, too, Jake."

He lets go of my hand after a quick shake, then scratches the underside of his jaw. "Don't forget what I said about the guarantee. And if Bren bothers you again, let me know. I'll take care of it."

You know what? I actually believe him, too.

"Thanks."

"Don't mention it. You have a nice day, okay?"

I'll try.

Surprisingly, I end up having a pretty great day after all. After I went back inside, I decided it was time to start painting. Hyperfocus can come in handy when it's on a project instead of something more detrimental to me—like shopping or even a person—and I had the whole living room taped off in no time.

The actual painting took a little longer, but I was determined to get it done in one day. So I threw my hair up in a ponytail, pulled on a tank top and shorts because I was already sweating, and got to work.

The thing about hyperfocusing is that it's all you can do. Nothing can stop you when you're in the middle of it. I think I took one bathroom break and had, like, three sips of water all day, but by the late afternoon, the entire living room was pink, and I'd only fucked up one spot.

I wanted to go over it again and fix it, but the fumes from the paint were starting to get to me. Realizing I never opened a window for ventilation because I was just too focused on getting the job done, I went to do that—and yelp when I find something waiting for me on the outer windowsill.

It's a pink rose. Not just the bloom or a few scattered petals like I've found in my house from time to time, but another full rose, including the stem.

I can't see if it has any thorns on it or leaves because a good chunk of the stem is covered in something white.

It takes me a minute before it hits me *why*.

Someone has wrapped a note around the stem, then left the flower in a place I'd obviously find it.

I've seen flowers like this before. I've gotten a note before, too, though that was left in my mailbox. Could this be from the same person? I don't know, and I can't figure out how he would've gotten it here without me seeing until I remember that hyperfocusing on a project makes me basically blind to everything but the task I'm working on.

For all I know, someone could've stood in front of the living room window and watched me all day, and I'd have no fucking clue.

I'd like to think my neighbors would notice, but I'm the only one who's really home during the day. The Fields have work and school, the Millers do, too, and both of the Douglases are constantly pulling long shifts. I saw my new neighbor head out to the garage earlier, too... so maybe someone could've been spying on me.

But *why*?

I don't know, but before I can think better of it, I

rush outside in my bare feet and snatch the rose off of the sill.

If there are any thorns, I don't feel them through the scrap of paper wrapped around it. With trembling fingers, I start to unroll it, sighing softly when I see that whoever put this rose here *did* take the time to hack off the thorns.

Then I unfold the scrap, reading the same blocky print and scrawled signature, and know exactly who it was.

The Watcher.

SIX

WILL AND THE WINDOW

SIMONE

"**W**here did you get those from?"

Will is back again, scowling at me from across the room. He's got a look of annoyance on his face as he glares at all of the roses I've laid out on my bed.

There are six. Anytime I found one—either on my dresser, by my front door, even in my *car*—I scooped it up and tossed it into my pajama drawer with everything else I've been trying to hide.

But after that second note, making it clear to me that the Watcher *is* really my stalker, I can't pretend any longer that the flowers and the strange messages meant for me aren't connected.

As soon as I dashed back into the house, Will was waiting for me. Of course he was. It was a replay of a scene we've had together too many times. Whenever I used to get bored with the apartment and he allowed me to change it up, I had to listen to him complain that the TV looked better over there or the paint wasn't even enough or why did I waste his money on a shelf like that...

So, yeah. My dead husband just had to pick apart my paint job from this afternoon. Then, when I purposely ignored him, heading to the kitchen to find something to eat to steady both my blood sugar and my nerves, he stood by the refrigerator, telling me that I could've found something healthier to snack on than a granola bar.

The ghost of my husband was quiet after I finished and went upstairs, searching for the other flowers, but once I had them laid out on my comforter, he started up once more.

And I'm fucking sick of it.

Barely glancing over at him, I snap, "Aren't you done with nagging me for the night?"

"Sorry, sweetheart, but I'm fucking dead. Worm food, right? I don't have anything better to do than visit my bride."

I snort. "I never should've married you."

"What's wrong, Simone? Would you have rather stuck it out with your ex? Married him instead?"

"Maybe," I lie.

Will calls my bluff. "Please. I thought he scared the shit out of you."

My high school sweetheart was a nice guy. A good guy. I don't think I realized how good I had it until I broke things off with him to go to college, then fell into Will's orbit.

"He didn't scare me," I tell him. "The commitment scared me. I was a kid. I wanted to see the world—"

"And didn't you? I took you to Italy for our honeymoon. Hawaii for our first anniversary. You can't tell me I didn't show you the damn world, you ungrateful bitch."

Ah, there it is. Will's 'sweetheart' one moment and his 'ungrateful bitch' the next. And he wonders why I secretly wished him dead these last few years.

I ignore him. When he was alive, Will *hated* that. He rarely got physical with me—if only because he knew he could wound just as hard with words, plus they didn't leave bruises that I had to lie to well-meaning bystanders about—but when he did, he blamed it on losing his temper whenever I didn't rise to his bait.

And, yes, I know I'm just ignoring myself right now... but that's fine. Besides, it's not like the ghost of my dead husband can really expect me to answer him, not about the trips he took me on to buy my happiness, or why I'm attached to a couple of wilting roses.

How can I when *I* don't know the answer?

Will's quiet for a few moments. It won't last; it never did when he was still alive. He'd either explode or grab me, shaking me, doing everything to get me to look at him. But he can't now. He's *dead*. Not even a real ghost who might be able to poltergeist me or something, he's a simple figment of my imagination who can't hurt me anymore than I can hurt myself.

Still, he's quiet, and that's not like the dead husband I keep imagining. I see why when I finally dare to lift my head up again and look over to where he was hovering.

He's gone. The room is empty. He completely disappeared.

"Will?"

No answer.

Am I getting better? Doing better?

Have I finally figured out a way to stop him from haunting me?

I hope so. I desperately want to move on. Will's dead. I can't change that. I'm not sure I would if I *could*. He got his revenge, right? The vision of his ghost has tormented me for months now... have I finally broken free of him?

I really fucking hope so.

"Will? You here?"

Nothing.

Yes...

I was sitting on my bed. Now that he's gone, if only for the moment—please don't let it be just for the moment—I slowly get up, walking to the other side of the room where he'd been before. Knowing it's silly but unable to stop myself, I run my hand through the space, rolling my eyes when it's obvious there's nothing there.

Okay. I think I've really lost it this time. I don't know if I ever had it, but I've certainly fucking lost it.

He's dead. Dead, dead, dead.

Get it through your skull, Simone.

Besides, there are real-life monsters still out there. People who *can* hurt you. People who don't go away because you ignore them for a while... people who might be watching you right now—

With a sigh, I turn, ready to go back to the flowers. For some reason, they comfort me, even if they shouldn't. Because they're pink? Because they're a sign of softness from a mysterious man whose first gift to me was covered in blood?

Your guess is as good as mine, but I haven't been able to throw any of them away yet...

Just as I turn, something catches my attention out of the corner of my eye. At first, I can't say what it is. It's out the window. I thought... I thought I saw something.

I move to stand in front of it. I wasn't wrong. There's a shadowy figure standing on the edge of the street, closer to my house. His head is angled up as though he's searching for me, willing me to come to the window.

Is it... is it Will?

I see him everywhere. Is he taunting me from outside of the house? I can't tell. The figure is a dark silhouette standing out against the shadows of the night, barely touched by any of the streetlights. He couldn't have picked a more perfect spot.

I need a better a look.

What the...

I press my forehead and my nose to the glass. That doesn't really help, but I can say one thing for sure: that's not Will.

I don't even know how I saw him. Dressed all in black, with something covering his face, the only thing I can see is a sliver of pale that might be his eyes, maybe, and something lighter that's clutched between his fingers.

My breath catches in my throat as he raises it up.

My hands are against the glass now. I'm paralyzed, unable to look away.

His arm moves. I think he's pulled something out of his pocket, but I can't tell what. He does it again, and now he has three things in his hands.

What are they?

I watch. I watch him watch me, the two of us in a stalemate until he takes a few steps toward my house. Shivers course down my spine as I realize what he's doing: he's heading right for my front door.

That gives me the strength I need to move away from the window. Shifting quickly, my back against the wall, I clutch the plaster with frantic fingers and I wait breathlessly for some sign that he's out there.

A knock. Why the fuck do I expect him to knock? I'm pretty sure it's too late for some kind of door-to-door salesman, and I never get deliveries once it's this dark out. Who is he? What does he want?

What was he holding?

There's no knock. No sign that he came to my house at all, and when I get the nerve to look out the window again, he's vanished as quickly as Will does.

But that wasn't Will.

Part of me wants to hop in my bed, send the flowers flying, yank the comforter over my head, and hide from whoever was out there. But the other part... the part that used to be scared, but absolutely refuses to be anymore... she tiptoes down the stairs, moves through the freshly painted living room, curses under her breath when she sees she forgot to close the window... and then, knowing she shouldn't but doing so anyway, she pulls open the front door.

I think I would've passed out on the spot if the face-less figure had been standing on my porch. He isn't, but there is something there.

And now I know what he was holding—and what he must've pulled out of his pocket.

Because there, on my porch, is another rose with its stem wrapped in paper.

I snatch it, bringing it inside where the light is better. Then, because I know better what to expect this time, I hurriedly unravel the paper—and when I read it, my hand flexes, and both the rose and the note flutter free from my grip.

That's okay. I don't think I'll forget what it says anytime soon...

At first, I was terrified.

I'll admit it. The Watcher's third note had a decidedly darker air to it; that's saying something considering the first one was accompanied by my dead husband's bloody wedding ring. But this one? It seems like a threat.

Don't look out the window? Why? Is he there?

Was that him?

What the hell is he hiding? What does he want with me?

The questions wouldn't stop. So consumed with the mystery of him, I'm too distracted to even hallucinate Will. It's just me left alone with my thoughts, and two days after he left that note on my doorstep, I'm no closer to figuring him out.

I ran right to the internet. All of the hits on the Watcher talked about a creepy dude who sent letters to a family in Westfield, New Jersey, all signed by 'The Watcher' in a cursive font. That was about a decade ago or so, with the letter-writer seemingly obsessed with the house.

Not my Watcher. He seems to be obsessed with *me*... and I can't live like this.

I *can't.*

Not knowing why he's out there. *When* he's out there.

Why me? Why did he pick *me*?

Was it because of Will? Or did whatever happen to Will happen because of me?

Who is he? Do I know him? Do I want to?

And what does he expect from me?

That last question is the one that haunts me the most; when Will doesn't, the reality of being a pretty woman with a target on her back makes that last one fucking obvious.

Consider yourself single... for now.

Is that it? He watches me—because that's what he's doing, standing out on the street, head tilted up to look in my window... watching—because he wants me?

Don't look out your window... you might not like what you see...

Maybe that's so. Or maybe I'm sick and fucking tired of men telling me what to do. They always have. My dad, moving the family around for his job no matter how we felt about it. My high school boyfriend who thought he could mold me into the perfect wife. Will, who sure as hell tried to do just that after college... I'm done. I'm fucking *done*.

It's my turn to take control of my life. Fuck Will Burke. Fuck the husband who won't leave me alone even after he got himself killed. Fuck the man who thinks he can intimidate me by stalking me, watching me, trying to *control* me.

Don't look out my window, huh? Two can play this game. Because if he's looking into my window now... maybe I should give him something *he*'d like to see.

"LOST CONTROL AND RANG YOUR BELL. I WAS SORE

LET ME IN OR ELSE I'LL BEAT DOWN YOUR DOOR..."

Silhouette, The Rays (1956)

SEVEN

INVITATION

JAKE

Squeezing my phone, glaring at what I'm seeing on the screen, I have only one thought: *what the fuck does Simone think she's doing?*

I'm used to her nighttime routine. Depending on if she showered earlier in the day or not, she'll hop into the stall if she needs to, or just wash her face at the sink before doing her skincare routine. She throws her hair into a messy ponytail at the top of her head, pulling on a pair of comfy-looking pajamas, then goes to bed.

One thing she doesn't do? Is strip down in her bedroom before heading toward the window.

But that's exactly what she just did.

I had a long day at work. Maybe I shouldn't have laced Brendon's latest jug of iced tea, but I couldn't

95

help myself after I finally moved on to the next step of my plan and introduced myself to Simone. I needed her to be aware of *Jake*, and after her trip to the garage, I used that as a perfect opportunity to talk to her.

Then I almost lost my fucking cool when my sweet vixen—perceptive as ever—called Brendon out on exactly what he did. No wonder she's so anxious that something else would happen to her beloved car. After messing with the window mechanism to get her down at Frank's in the first place, I've left it alone—but the damage was done.

It's up to me to fix it.

I tried. I told her about the guarantee, then, in a burst of inspiration, made sure she knew she could come to me if she thought Brendon was still bothering her. After the first bout of uncontrollable diarrhea, I would've thought he got the message, but to be sure, I gave him another.

Fucking backfired on me, didn't it? Once, he could blow off as food poisoning. But twice? He's not quick enough—or twisted enough—to jump to being *actually* poisoned by someone he knows and stupidly trusts, but he'd be a much bigger idiot not to think that something's wrong.

So he called off today to see his doctor. And while I'm not worried about what his PCP's gonna say, it left me and Manny to do all the work down at the garage. Manny's only an apprentice, too, with his nose so far up Frank's ass, it has a permanent brown spot on it.

He was no help, and I cleared all the tickets on my own.

All I wanted to do was have a cold beer, kick off my boots, and watch Simone sleep. On my good days, I'll sneak out, break in through the back door, and do so from inside of her closet so that she doesn't wake up to find me staring at her. Tonight? It's not one of my good days.

I'm a cocktail of exhaustion and frustration, and while I'd like to think I've learned some control when it comes to my girls, I'm not so sure it's a good idea for me to be so close to Simone tonight.

If there's one thing I can say about myself, it's that I never take what I'm not given.

I'm obsessive. I think laws are for other people. Stupid people who can't find ways around them. That doesn't mean I don't have my own moral code, though. I never killed before—not even when Scott tried to convince Casey to break up with me so he could take her to prom—until Will Burke pushed my hand. I let him survive even when I knew he was going home and fucking *my* sweet vixen, and I would've let him be after she left him because losing Simone... I can't think of any worse fate.

But he didn't just hurt her. He was obsessed to the point that he would've stolen her from me *permanently* if I let him. So I couldn't let him. He had to die, and as easy as it was to kill him, I'd rather not do that again if I don't have to.

So I watch Simone, but I don't touch. I'll jerk off to her pictures and the video on my phone, smiling to myself when I think of her wearing my semen in her hair after she washes it... and that's it. I never want to put myself into a situation where I cross the line from obsessed stalker to something I can't come back from—

—but now I have no choice.

Simone is standing in front of her window. The shade is up. So is the glass. Nothing can stop anyone from seeing her naked body as she skims her hands up her side, cupping her breasts.

The camera in her room is angled so that all I can see is her slender back, but I can tell from the movements that that is just what she's doing.

Fuck *no*.

Jumping to my feet, clutching my phone in my hand, I race for the front of my house, angling my head out of my own window. And I'm right. With the light on in her room, she's a silhouette against it, hiding all of the details... but there's no denying that she's both gloriously naked and caressing herself seductively.

Oh, Simone... you don't know what you've done, have you?

Or maybe she has. I warned her. In the note I left her... I've seen her peering out her window, staring forlornly out onto the street so many times that it's a miracle she hasn't seen me until now. And since I knew she wasn't ready to confront me yet—to confront the reality that I'm hers and she's mine—I gave her the option to look away.

But she didn't. Instead, she's made me jealous of *myself*.

This little show she's putting on... Simone isn't doing this for Jake McIntyre.

She wants the Watcher's attention. She wants the figure she caught spying on her the other night. The man I let her see because I did want her to know I was out there. That I *was* watching.

That she's mine...

If this is how she decided to respond to my note, then message received, Simone.

She wants the Watcher?

I'll give her him.

———

Simone's gone from the window by the time I'm slipping out of the back door of my house. All I can think is *good* because for all my talk about not wanting to kill again, I might have had to change my mind if one of our neighbors caught a glimpse of something that was meant for my eyes only.

I'm suddenly crazed regardless. I can't get the image of her squeezing her tits out of my head, and it makes me reckless. I almost bolt across the street in my hurry to get to her, holding myself back just in time. This is different. This is a *dare*. As much as I want to,

I'm not about to fuck this chance up by running over to her house and banging on her front door.

Tonight? Screw being exhausted. I'm alert now, my brain whirring, and I tell myself that this requires subtlety. *Skill.* I've spent months working toward this moment, learning Simone, showing her that I'm the one and only man who deserves her...

Whether she meant to summon the possessive bastard dying to own her with her little show or not, it doesn't matter. That's exactly what she did—and I'm coming for her.

The silent trek through the woods seems impossibly long tonight. I'm alone in the darkness, the sound of my pulse racing, the blood rushing straight to my cock my only companion as the rest of the cul de sac better fucking be asleep.

Tonight is for Simone and her Watcher, that's it.

Eventually, she'll know that she's always been meant for *Jake.* Instead of a conversation full of small talk by her Mazda, I'll grab her by the ponytail, arch her back, and fuck her so deeply, she'll be panting *my* name, spilling all of her deepest, darkest secrets to Jake McIntyre.

Only then will I finally be able to shed the nice guy mask that's gotten me to this point, going so far as to get rid of the collection of black balaclavas I habitually yank on to hide my identity whenever I'm outside watching her.

No one's seen me yet. No one *ever* sees me...

She won't, either, tonight. Not the way I wish she could, but that's imperative. It's also the next step of my plan, even if I'm adjusting it on the fly.

Simone might not be drawn to Jake just yet. If I can get her addicted to the Watcher, that'll come in time. It'll have to.

Fuck me, but I swear I'll be whoever I have to be to make my sweet vixen *mine*...

She already belongs to the Watcher. That little display tells me so—as well as the way she left her back door *unlocked*.

Was it on purpose? Every fucking time I've let myself into her sanctuary, I've needed the set of burglary tools I keep in my back pocket to unlock the door first. My Simone can be a bit absent-minded sometimes, but she's never, ever left her home or her car open.

Look at that, I think, smiling to myself as I pull my mask on. Another invitation.

I slip into her kitchen, careful to lock the door behind me for both of our sakes. Cocking my head, I hear the rush of water above me, the groan of the water heater coming from the back room, and my smile widens a little more.

Simone is taking a shower.

No—she's giving me one final invitation.

Oh, baby. You don't have to ask me twice.

I remove my boots, lining them up by the back door. A pang of satisfaction rushes through me when I see them there. They belong in Simone's house. So do I, but since I don't hold out much hope that this invitation will extend to forever just yet, I undress quickly, then fold up my clothes so that they're within reach on my way out of her house.

My cock is so hard, I almost want to take a minute to jerk off just so that I won't embarrass myself in front of Simone. I've spent months wondering what it would be like to see her naked in the flesh, and even if nothing else happens tonight, that will.

Now I want to touch her. Just touch her. Let my fingertips learn the shape and texture of her skin. That's all. I'm not greedy.

Nope. I just want everything she is, 'til death do *we* part.

Simone is a silhouette on the shower curtain when I ease open the bathroom door and, stepping on the balls of my feet, move into the room.

It's full of steam. The mirror is fogged over, the heated wisps carrying the undeniable scent of *Simone* over to me as I take a moment to breathe it in.

She's humming softly as the water sprays. I'm careful to close the door without a click so that I don't disturb her. For all of my interpreting her actions as an open invitation to the Watcher, I'm prepared to talk her down in case I frighten her.

I should've known better. When the shower curtain crinkles as I pull it far enough to slip my body into the tub with her, she goes absolutely still, but she doesn't scream.

Instead, in a breathless tone, she asks softly, "Is someone there?"

Now that I've introduced myself to her as Jake, it's time for her to meet the Watcher. And though it kills me to admit that this woman—the object of my desire, my love, my affection, my *obsession*—probably won't recognize my voice without seeing my face, I don't want to take any chances.

I can't. Not until I have her so completely obsessed with me in return that she'll willingly do anything Jake *or* the Watcher demands of her.

For the moment, I think only the Watcher has any sway over her, and I'm going to use that to my advantage while I can.

So I simply lower my voice, making it gruffer than usual, and answer her with a simple, "*Yes.*"

My brave girl stuns me with her reaction. As though she can already sense that she's safe with me, she only gulps, then turns away from the shower spray so that she's facing me.

She gasps when she sees the mask. Almost as if on their own, her hands start to reach up for the hem of the balaclava.

That's a hard no from me. The mask covers my entire head and throat with only one long hole cut out for my eyes. Forget being able to see. I picked this mask because I want her to look at me and know—just *know* —that she's staring up at Jake McIntyre. There's no recognition in her sad brown eyes, though. Just surprise and, unless I'm fucking willing into existence, *excitement.*

She reached for me. It's only fair I get to do the same.

My fingers land lightly on the sides of her damp, slick neck. She jolts, but before she can do anything else, I grate out, "If you try to peel off my mask, I'll go."

Simone gulps. I trail my thumb down the front column of her throat, too late to catch her sudden fear.

Maybe it's better this way. She *should* be afraid of what a faceless, nameless man can do to her when she's at her most vulnerable. If I wasn't the one lucky enough to see the outline of her naked body before she walked away from the window, who else might have decided to take advantage of my sweet vixen?

I love her, but she doesn't love me yet. She doesn't *know* me yet. That'll change in time, when the Watcher becomes Jake—or Jake is revealed to be the Watcher— but, for now, her fear will make her easy to control.

So will her undeniable lust.

I sense it all around me. The fear mingled with need, the slight hitch in her breath that tells me she's more intrigued by my presence than terrified. Her fingers are trembling, mere inches away from my side.

She wants to touch me. She wants me to touch her.

Even if a part of her would insist that she doesn't... I know Simone.

After all, my pretty blonde girl is the one who teased me. Who invited me in with nothing more than a pointed stare out of her window and the shape of her body, a sight meant solely for the twisted man she had to know was watching her...

She swallows again, inching closer. Her fingers brush against my damp side as she whispers, "Is that all it takes? I go for your mask and you'll leave? As simple as that?"

Not for the reasons she think, but—

"Yes."

I mean it. I want nothing more than to pleasure this woman, even if the extent of all I get to experience tonight is the simple act of sharing a shower with Simone. But if she crosses this one boundary with me, forcing my hand the same time as she rushes my plan, I'll have no choice but to go back to the shadows. The Watcher will do what he does, while Jake will do whatever he can to catch Simone's attention instead.

It would surprise everyone I've known, including my cousin, but I've learned some patience over the last few years. I've learned to work hard for what I want, to lay a trap, to be able to *wait*. Now, Simone being drawn to the Watcher isn't something I'd anticipated and, fuck yeah, I'll take any chance to get closer to her... but Simone and me... we're endgame, no matter what.

Jake and Simone. Whatever it takes, whatever it

costs, whatever I have to do... I will have this woman on her knees, but though I'd give anything I fucking have to drop my hands to her hips, turn her around, bend her over, and fuck her so completely that she'll forever miss it whenever my dick isn't nestled inside of her where it belongs, I stay still.

Even as her gaze dips low enough to notice my cock straining for her. Even as she hitches another breath, two fingertips ghosting near my hip bone as though she senses that clutching me, pulling me toward her is just what she should do... even as her tongue darts out, swiping the corner of her mouth as the shower spray trickles down her cheeks... I don't move a fucking muscle.

Well, except for my wayward erection. It twitches, crying out for Simone, and her soft breath wafting toward me on the warm air is enough to make me almost spill at her feet.

I've learned patience, but it fucking sucks to wait. Still, I stay silent as I leave the ball in her court. What will she do?

Her eyes are trained on my cock. It's angry and it's red, so damn hard that it's undeniable that I'm aching for her, and she doesn't react for what seems like a goddamn lifetime.

Then she does, and I have to clench my teeth to keep from spitting out a curse.

Simone draws her hands away from me. I watch her fingers tremble before she balls them into fists, taking a few hesitant steps away from me. She puts as much space between us as she can while we're both standing together in the shower—but she still doesn't scream. I'm more than ready to bend her over and take her in this shower stall, she fucking *knows* it, and she doesn't scream.

I want to say that I expected that. That the Simone I know would be curious about a masked man showing up *naked* in her bathroom... but that would be a lie. I wasn't thinking when I took her up on her invitation, and if I was, I'd have been sure that her first instinct would be to run away.

It isn't. There's distance between us now, sure, but though her eyes meet mine now, it isn't long before they dip back to my cock.

Yes...

Simone swallows again. Could be fear. Could be lust. Could be a combination of the two—

"You... you're naked."

It's not an accusation. Fuck no. That tone in her voice... it's a *revelation.*

I've learned patience. I swear to God that I have. But when I hear that wonder... if I don't do something to show this woman that I didn't just come by to rinse off, I might explode.

I won't push her. This is already going better than I expected, and if I *push*, she might run out of here, wet and terrified. No. She has nothing to be afraid of —not while I'm around—and this is my chance to prove to her that the Watcher isn't just her silent shadow.

He's her stalker *and* her savior.

Instead of crowding her, covering her body with mine while I back her up against the tile, I ease a few steps closer to Simone.

Reaching out my hand again, I ghost the back of my fingers against one pebbled nipple. I'm not touching her, not quite, though the heat from my hand mingling with the heat from the shower spray has her arching her back enough that she brushes against me.

She touches *me*.

Beneath my mask, I grin. "So are you." Fuck it. She touched me first. She gave me access to her body whether she meant to or not. Way I see it, that's just more permission...

Turning my hand, cupping her tit, I give her a gentle squeeze. "Just like you were in the window."

She doesn't draw away from me. She stands there, breathing so heavily now that the weight of her perfect-sized tit shifts against my callused palm, but doesn't make any effort to get me to let her go.

Good. My sweet vixen is already learning.

I will *never* let her go.

EIGHT

CONTROL

JAKE

Simone hesitates for a moment before she murmurs, "You saw that?"

"You meant for me to."

Simone doesn't say anything to that. She just bites down on her bottom lip as her eyes dip between the few inches I've left between us, dropping down to my cock again.

Honestly, I don't think she even seems to realize that I'm still holding her tit in my hand. So stunned—or maybe entranced—by my hard-on and how it's close enough to nudge her hip, she can't keep her eyes off of it.

And I've never been so fucking excited in my life.

This is exactly the kind of reaction I was hoping for

from my Simone. No more fear. That's already slipping away, going down the drain the same as the gathered water running beneath our bare feet. No trepidation, either. Just pure animalistic *want* between two souls who are made for each other.

I'm coiled up with it myself, so tight I'm ready to explode. One touch. It took my fingers grazing her soft skin for the first time to know that all of the long nights, the hectic move out of my parents house in Springfield and into this empty one here in Merrill Grove, the new job, the blood on my hands... it was worth it for this single moment in time with Simone.

But, fuck it, I *am* greedy. I need more. I *want* more.

And, more than anything in this world, I need her to want it, too.

She'll come to her senses soon. The two of us... we're standing on the precipice of something huge. One wrong push and we can go tumbling over the side, but if I ease her into this...

We can both get what we want—and deserve.

Releasing her tit, I immediately trail my hand up her jaw before cupping that next. I use a little pressure to tilt her head back so that she's looking at me.

I shudder just enough when I see all of the emotions lurking in the depths of her sad brown eyes. How much she's torn between bolting and staying, ripping off my mask and letting it stay in place so that I don't go—and so that she can pretend that she had no choice.

If she wants to make me shoulder all of the responsibility for what comes next, I'll take that weight gladly. I won't force her, but if that's what she needs from the Watcher, I'll give it to her.

I'll give her everything, but only if she understands this *one* thing—

"I won't hurt you," I promise in that deep voice. "Before anything else, I need you to know that, Simone. Tell me you understand."

Give me permission to do whatever I want to and say *yes*...

This is important to me. I won't scare her away if I can help it. I won't allow her to be another Casey. I even learned from the mistakes I made with Heather, too. She had to die, but I made sure to kill the biggest threat to my sweet vixen before Burke could even try to take Simone away from me.

I'll own the blood on my hands, but for all the responsibilities I'll take on when it comes to this woman, I won't be the reason why another pretty blonde with sad brown eyes dies. Not this time. Definitely not this one. Simone will always be mine, and there isn't anything I won't do to get her to understand that and agree.

She hesitates. I'd expected as much, but I refuse to release her chin even as she tilts her head back, meeting my gaze straight-on again.

"How can I?"

It would be so much easier if she just said 'yes', but us McIntyres... when have we ever gotten off on easy?

How can she believe me?

"You can't," I tell her honestly. "You'll have to trust me."

Simone lets out a sound that's half laugh, half sob, jerking her head out of my hold. I let her because that sound... damn it, I might've already pushed her too far.

"Are you serious? Trust the intruder who broke into my house? Into my *shower*? Who knows my name... touches me like he has the right... but won't even let me see his face?"

She's not wrong. But if she wants to pretend like I just decided to add a little B&E to my record...

"You could've locked the back door."

I wait for her to tell me it was a mistake. An accident. That she never would've left it open for me on purpose—

Simone gives her head a royal shake, spraying water in my face as her wet hair falls down her back. She lifts her chin a little higher. "Would that have kept you out?"

Not even a little, and my silence answers the question for her.

We're mere inches away again. Our bodies are slick from the shower, her breasts heaving now, my own chest doing something similar. The only thing coming between us right now is the water falling from the shower head above us.

I don't mean to back her in, to cover her smaller form with my body, but if she's going to bolt, she's going to have to get through me to do so.

For a moment, I don't think she realizes that I've trapped her in the corner of the stall. When she rips her gaze from me, glancing around, I'm sure she does now. Sorry, baby. I'm ready to do anything to stop her from escaping me, not when I still haven't gotten her word that she knows instinctively that she's safe with me.

I'll take her. I'll own her. I'll keep her for the rest of my life—but I'll never hurt her, and it's so fucking important to me that she admits she understands that I'll keep her in this stall until the water freezes both of us before I ever let her escape me in this charged moment.

But Simone doesn't want to escape. Because, to my surprise, she moves her naked body into mine and plants her hands on my chest.

The unexpected contact steals nearly all of my control from me. I don't grab her, though I do groan— and she narrows her gaze at the sound.

"Who are you?" Simone demands. It comes out breathlessly, and the only reason I don't grab her and press her body against mine is because I already caged her in with my arms.

I dig my fingers against the slick title of her bathroom wall. Who am I? What the hell kind of question is that?

She has to know. She invited me in here... she *has* to know.

Right?

I look down at her, knowing all she can see now is the drenched black mask conforming to my features and the heat in my eyes as I ask, "Don't you know?"

The defiance that twists her lips into a small smile has me seconds away from nutting all over her. I won't waste my jizz, can't waste it when she's so close, but I'm on the edge of losing any control I might still have when she murmurs softly, "I want to hear you say it."

That's my good girl. Smart, too. Just like I thought, she knows exactly who I am—who she invited into her home—but she wants to make sure that her masked man is who she was expecting.

One hand stays on the wall, bracing my weight so that I don't fall on her like I want to. The other goes to her cheek, wiping a stray bead of water away from the height of it. She's tucked behind the shower spray now, letting most of it fall on me, traveling in rivulets down my hard chest, but when she shivers, I want to believe it's from my touch rather than missing the warmth of the water.

"I'm the Watcher," I rumble back at her.

"Yeah?" It's a whisper now. "And what do you watch?"

Oh, Simone... it's not a 'what', and we both know that. "I watch *you*."

Her lips part.

Her lips part, and I don't even know if she says anything because my blood is suddenly pounding in my ears. You'd think most of it would be in my cock by now, but nope. I hear the *thud*, feel my heart racing as all I want to do is ravage that mouth.

I'm not picky. I could push down on her shoulders, guiding her to her knees, and feed my cock past those gorgeously plump limps. I could even play the part of a gentleman, lift my mask up just enough to free my own mouth, and kiss her the way I've spent months dreaming of.

But I don't. Taking her mouth in any way would be a slippery fucking slope. First her mouth, then her pussy, and I'd make Simone mine in this shower without giving a shit about tomorrow.

If I only wanted one night with her, I would. But fuck that. I'm playing the long game here. I want forever, and if that means taking that last kernel of control I've got and hanging onto it, I will.

I'm not mad at Simone for being so fucking tempting, but tell that to the way my voice comes out as a bark as I demand her to, "Turn around."

She jolts. From the sound, from the command, or because I'd interrupted whatever the hell she was saying, I don't know. But she jolts, suddenly frightened, and leans back agains the wall. "What—"

Fuck. Some control. I scared her and that just won't fucking do.

"I mean it, Simone. Turn around." Then, purposely

gentling my tone even as I continue to try and disguise it, I promise, "I won't hurt you. I fucking swear it. I just wanna take care of you."

"How?"

"Turn around. Face the water." It kills me to back away, but if I need her to trust me, I have to show her that I trust her first. "Come over here."

She swallows, and when her eyes dart toward the shower curtain, I wonder if she's gonna finally run. She doesn't. Instead, doing what I asked, she shuffles across the tub, turning and angling her head so that the water is spraying down on her chest.

"Good girl," I murmur. "Now stay there."

"What are you—" she begins again.

I reach behind me, grabbing her shampoo bottle. "You'll see."

After I pour a bunch of the shampoo into my palm, I rub it through Simone's hair, lathering it, then scrubbing her scalp. She's tense at first, most likely because she can't miss my cock jabbing her in the lower back as I turn all of my attention to washing her hair, but once she realizes that I didn't have her turn around so that I could take her from behind, she relaxes just enough for it to be noticeable.

I help Simone rinse out the shampoo, then once she's facing the shower spray again, I go for the conditioner.

I just want to pamper her right now. To show her that she can believe me when I say I won't hurt her, and to pleasure her in all the ways she deserves, not just with sex. Gonna be honest, though, and say that I'm so damn glad her back is to me again—and that my mask is covering most of my face—because I'd probably scare the shit out of her with how possessively I'm staring as I rub the conditioner into her hair now.

My sweet vixen has no idea I've marked it—that I've marked *her* for almost two months now—but it does something to me to apply the come-filled conditioner to her hair myself.

Now, I could've stopped there. But as she lets out a soft moan as I scrub her scalp with the conditioner now, I admit that there are limits to even the last of my lingering self-control.

Tugging the shower curtain open, I lean my body out of the tub so that I can root around the small wooden basket she keeps on the metal rack over her toilet.

"Are you leaving?" Simone suddenly asks, only hearing the whisper of the plastic moving since she can't see what I'm doing with her back still to me. "I didn't touch your mask. You know I didn't."

Holy shit. She *wants* me to stay. I can hardly fucking believe it, but Simone is trying to tell me why I don't have a reason to leave her right now... which is a good thing because I'm not going anywhere.

"Just grabbing a washcloth, my sweet vixen. That's all."

I grab one, then close the shower curtain behind us

just in time for her to ask, "What is that you keep calling me? Sweet vixen... isn't that, like, an oxymoron?"

Maybe. I don't know. It's just the way I've always thought of Simone ever since I saw her with those tear-filled eyes outside of the Springfield convenience store. It popped into my head and never left, just like my obsession for this woman.

"It's my pet name for you."

"Like you're the Watcher."

"If that's how you want to think of it. But you can call me anything you want, baby, as long as it's *yours*."

Shit. She stiffens up again even as the last of the conditioner streams out of her hair.

Finally, in a voice so quiet I can hardly hear it over the shower, she whispers, "But why? I have to ask. That's what I really want to know. Why? Why me?"

Just like when it came to my name, I thought she *did*? That it was obvious, and maybe it was... to me. Not to Simone.

I grab her body wash from the shelf in her shower. As I open it up, plopping a large drop of the pink gel onto the washcloth, I tell her honestly, "Because I love you."

"Love me? You don't even know me."

That's what you think, baby.

It might be fucking devious to distract her with my words the same time as I start running the washcloth over her skin, touching every part of her I can reach under the guise of scrubbing her clean with the body wash, but I don't care. She let me wash her hair. She can let me wash *her,* too.

And all it will cost me is a little of the information I've learned about her these last few months...

"Let's see... I know your favorite drink is ginger ale. You'll only eat pizza with onion on it, but you hate the way the taste lingers, so you'll chew gum." The washcloth skims over her breast while I lean in, my mouth next to her ear as I whisper, "Cinnamon. It has to be cinnamon."

It's more of a hiss than anything. It tickles her skin, making her shiver despite the warmth in the shower.

"You're addicted to 90s sitcoms because, for some reason, you think life was better back then. But you'd never survive without your Amazon Prime, baby, so I don't know who you're fooling." The washcloth goes lower, circling her belly button. "Not me, for sure. Not with the fifteen boxes you get every week. And that's just Amazon. Don't get me started on the other stores you can't get enough of."

Simone shakes her head, though she doesn't shift away from me, not even as I move the hand holding the washcloth around her hip, stroking her ass—then drop the washcloth, too. "How did... are you stalking me?"

That's putting it mildly.

"You are my life, Simone. My *obsession.* Call it

stalking if you want. I like to think of it as...mmm... watching."

"Watching? I—" Simone stops, suddenly realizing that it's my bare finger that's currently easing its way through the slick wetness of her pussy. "What are you doing?"

"Getting you clean, baby. We're taking a shower together, and you're impossibly *wet*. Gotta make sure you're clean all over before we can... dry you off."

She reaches behind me, clutching my arm. "Your finger is about to go inside of me."

She doesn't say no. She doesn't try to tell me to stop. In fact, I'm pretty sure she's gone up on the balls of her feet, angling herself perfectly so that I have easier access to fingerfuck her if that's what I want to do.

And, God, do I fucking *want*.

Shit. I didn't come into the shower with her tonight, planning on giving her such an intimate touch so soon. I'd thought I'd make a point, take her up on her invitation, get her used to the idea of the Watcher first... but if she's into it? Why shouldn't I give my Simone everything she desires?

I trace the circle of her entrance with my pointer finger. "I said all over, didn't I?"

"*Watcher...*"

It's not my name. It shouldn't pain me as much as it does that she's not calling me by my name, not when I call her 'my sweet vixen'—or when she only knows me by my pseudonym. But, fuck me, once again I'm jealous of myself, and jealous Jake can be rash, reckless, and impulsive—and he proves that by running his finger up Simone's slit again before taking his hand back.

She gasps as though missing my touch, but before she can back her ass into me, I grab her wrist. One jerk of her hand and I have her palm angled so that I can press my cock against her delicate skin.

"Touch me." It's a ragged command, and one that's out before I even knew what I was going to say.

"What? No. I... I can't."

Yes. She *can*.

"Fine. Then tell me to go. If you really want to convince me that you haven't been eyeing my cock since I joined you in here tonight, tell me to leave and I'll fucking leave. But if you can't do that, Simone, then *touch me*."

I'm playing with fire. All it will take is her getting the nerve to refuse me and I'll have lost any progress I've made with her in the last few minutes.

Well, the *Watcher* will have...

Is that why I'm pushing her now? Because I'm ready to rip off this damn mask, show Simone *my* face, and make her understand that she's going to belong to Jake McIntyre?

Sure, it's possible—or I might have just thrown Royce's advice right out the window instead. I mean, look at us. I haven't gotten the chance to be the nice guy and ask Simone out on a date yet, but I'm naked, she's naked, and, holy fucking shit, after turning into me so that we're facing each other, she *is* touching me.

I don't know who shudders more visibly: me or Simone.

This is exactly what I dreamed of. Her light grip could be bit more possessive, but I can work with that. The fact that she closed her fingers around the base of my cock on her own is good enough for me for the moment.

Only one thing would make it better, and as I start to thrust in Simone's hand, spreading my legs, bracing my hand against the slick shower wall again so that I don't slip and fall on my bare ass... as I start rocking, fucking her fist, my eyes nearly roll to the back of my head as she follows my rhythm and moves with me.

I don't expect to last. I was already so close just by being near her. Having her hands on me? I hold out as long as I can so that she doesn't think sex with me will be a waste of time, but when I'm seconds away from doing just that, I grip her by the hips, stunning her as I trap her hand and my cock between our bodies.

I grunt out a release, painting the swell of Simone's lower belly with my come without wasting a single fucking drop.

Then, before she can try to back off and rinse the proof of my lust for her away with the water, I use the heel of my hand to rub it in.

She blinks up at me when I finally step back, giving her as much space as I can allow. "What the..."

"You're mine, Simone. Just a little reminder. Try to run. Try to hide. I will find you. And when you're ready to accept that you've always been mine, let me know. Give me a sign, baby. I'll be there."

I'm *always* there.

NINE
HIS ATTENTION

He's gone as quickly as he came—both figuratively and literally.

As soon as the Watcher rubs his come into my skin, I expect him to return the favor. I got him off, right? The least he could do was go back to what he started, touching my pussy until I orgasmed all over his hand. If I'd lost my mind long enough to give my masked stalker a handjob, I'll stay crazy a couple of minutes more so he can get me off, too.

But he doesn't. Still wearing his soaked mask, he drops a kiss to my forehead. I feel it through the fabric, hands landing on his sculpted chest one more time as I just about fall into him. He sucks in a breath, moans my name just once, and then he's *gone*.

I almost follow him. I probably could've. He

needed to grab the clothes he discarded, and unless the Watcher is also a flasher, he would've gotten dressed before leaving my house. I had plenty of time to hop out of the shower, grab a towel, and demand to know what the hell is going on.

Who is he?

What does he mean when he says he loves me?

And, most importantly, what happened to Will?

All pretty damn valid questions that it never occurred to me to ask when I had him naked, hot, and hard in the shower with me—and I don't know what the hell that says about me, but it's probably not anything good.

Because I love you...

I almost follow him, but I don't. I can't. My legs are shaky, my body aching from the way he touched me so masterfully before pulling away, demanding I take hold of his dick instead. My boobs are impossibly heavy right now. I swear to God, my nipples are so hard, I could poke an eye out. Leaving the sanctuary of the steamy shower, knowing I'll have to confront my actions—and *his*—when I do... I stay under the spray until the water goes cold, my lust is a little more manageable, and the Watcher would have had enough time to slip back out into the night.

I finish my shower alone. He washed my hair for me, scrubbing part of my front and back with the washcloth, but I still needed to wash my lower half. I take care of my legs and my feet, gasping when I brush my swollen clit with the washcloth. I'm so fucking horny it hurts, and I give myself a quick wash before rinsing off.

Not my stomach, though. If only for tonight, I like the idea of leaving his spunk right where he left it. The streaming water washed off some of it anyway. The rest can stay until I shower again tomorrow.

Maybe by then I'll get my head out of my dark fantasies and realize just how insane it is that I was intimate with the man who admitted he's my stalker.

My stalker—and the most obvious suspect in my husband's likely murder.

That's a splash of water in my face that's even colder than the shower. I'm trembling a little by the time I turn the knob off, easing gently out of the tub before reaching for a towel. I notice that one of my pink set is missing, and it makes me smile a little to think of the Watcher drying off with it.

I trade my towel for the fuzzy pink robe I ordered from the internet the other day. After running my brush through my hair, not bothering to throw it up in a ponytail so that it can air dry, I tighten my robe, take a deep breath, and leave the bathroom.

Is he still here? I don't... I don't *sense* anyone else in the house. Of course, that doesn't mean shit. The only way to know for sure if he left is by checking the house out by myself.

He's not in my room. Not in the spare room, either. Heading downstairs, my heart lodges in my throat as I go down the hall, peeking into the living room first before walking into the kitchen.

I pause, staring at the table.

My towel is there. Folded up neatly, placed in the middle of the table, I smile to see that he left my towel behind; I was pretty sure the Watcher would've taken it with him as some kind of a trophy. But there's something else, too. Tip-toeing into the kitchen, I gasp when I see the pink rose left on top of a scrap of paper.

Welp. There goes any idea that the pink roses I kept finding were blowing in through the window somehow. They've had to have been a gift from the Watcher all along.

Damn it. Next time Will pops in, I'm gonna get another lecture from my dead husband about how he's always right, and I'll forever be wrong...

I set the rose aside. Grabbing the paper, I see that it has writing on it. *Distinct* writing. From the all-caps print to the name scrawled at the bottom, even if I doubted that the man I pleasured isn't the same one as the man who sent me Will's ring, this would definitely set me straight.

It's another note from *him*, and it says:

How did he know? That I had every intention of laying back on my bed, legs spread, touching myself to the memory of his gruff voice and the powerful way he touched me before commanding me to do the same to him... how did he know that I was going to give myself the orgasm he denied me, even though a part of me was so caught up in the heat of the moment that, if he bent me over, I would've welcomed him fucking me?

How did he know? Because he's the Watcher, and he thinks he knows *everything* about me.

At least, that's what he wants me to believe. Impossible. I don't care how much you spy on me, *stalk* me, there are secrets that I'll take to my grave. Things that not even my husband knew, and anyone who might have, I've long cut myself off from already.

He knows the Simone he *wants* to know, and he thinks he can tell her what to do and she'll listen.

Don't touch my pussy...

His pussy, huh? He certainly fingered it like he owns it, but it's going to take more than that before he's able to claim it—to claim *me*—as his.

I'll be watching...

I'm sure he will. He already proved that tonight, coming right over after I bared my tits in the window. There's a good chance any of my neighbors might have gotten a show, too, but if the Watcher was out there... and he obviously wants me to believe that he's *always* watching... I thought that might be enough to tempt him.

Do I know *how* he's watching me? The paranoid side of me has me looking suspiciously in every corner, checking to see if there's some kind of camera in this house. It's not mine. Not really. I'm just renting it, and I don't know anything about the previous tenants or the landlords. There might be cameras, and if there are?

I'll be watching...

He'll know. If I disobey him, he'll know. And while I'd like to think that might be enough for my masked stalker to make a return trip to my place, what if it does the obvious? What if it turns him off and he punishes me by staying away?

Do I *want* him to stay away?

I don't know. I should say 'yes', but since the answer is probably a 'no', I just take a deep breath and tell myself that, fuck, I don't know. But it's enough that, as twisted up as I am, needing release, I don't slip my hand under my robe. I tighten the sash instead, fisting the note before turning around and heading for the stairs.

I don't stop until I'm standing in the same spot I was... shit. Was that only twenty minutes ago? Maybe thirty? My whole life flipped upside down in the time it would take to stream a fucking sitcom on TV.

Bracing my hands on my windowsill, I peer out into the street in front of my house. It's dark. A few houses are completely black, while a handful—including Jake's across from mine, and the Millers two houses down—have one or two lights still on like I do.

It's quiet. Calm. How much do you want to bet that none of my neighbors have any idea that a masked man with a body built for sin joined me in my shower and nutted all over my back?

But someone does. Someone knows.

He's out there. Somewhere.

Watching.

And as I grab my shade, tugging it down, I know that not even that will stop him.

I DIDN'T REALIZE HOW MUCH I MASTURBATE UNTIL I catch myself every time I'm about to slip my hand through the folds of my pussy. As though I'm being shocked before I can use the tip of my finger to rub my clit, I think of *him* and yank my hand away.

It's ridiculous. I know it is. Even if he does have

cameras in here, it's not like he can see what I'm doing under a blanket. I'd like to think my shower's off-limits, too, but who knows?

It's been almost a week since I saw him. Since I proved to myself that he was real. Instead of just looking over my shoulder for my dead husband, now I'm expecting to find a toned body wearing nothing but a mask—only I haven't. Just like Will, it seems like the Watcher has vanished.

I don't know how to feel about that. Maybe that quick shower was all he needed from me. I gave him what he wanted when he pushed his dick into my hand. So he said he was watching... I'm watching back and, unlike before, I can't find him out there in the shadows of the street.

What's even stranger to me is that no one else has. I've asked. Ruby's husband Mark is head of our local neighborhood watch, and when I saw him taking the trash out the other day, I struck up a conversation, wondering if he'd heard anything about strangers lurking around our street, playing pranks or messing around by wearing a mask. He seemed concerned at my question, but assured me that he would've heard about that if it was the case.

Then he asked me if I had a report to make. I quickly brushed him off, passing it as a rumor I heard from the Field twins who live on the other side of me. Two very curious eight-year-olds, they're the darlings of the cul de sac, and just as nosy as Mark's wife.

They're still kids, though, and the childfree Mr. Douglas smiled indulgently at me when I told him that I got my intel from the twins.

I felt bad about lying, but it's not like it was the first time I've done so. My life's been built upon a pyramid of fabrications and untruths so, really, what was one more? Especially when I got what I wanted: confirmation that either I imagined the Watcher the same way I do Will, or he's just really that fucking good of a stalker.

I have to lean toward the second because, even in my messed-up brain, I don't think I could imagine a body as delicious as the Watcher's...

One good thing about the Watcher stepping out of the darkness—whether he's real or not—is how much more *comfortable* I am in leaving my house. It's almost like I don't want him to think he scares me or allow him to control my life; keeping my hands out of my panties the only exception. The cul de sac is a cozy community, and I'm starting to actually talk to my neighbors instead of high-tailing it into my house whenever someone else opens their door.

I know that the girl Field twin likes to dance, while her brother does soccer. The Millers go away to visit Mr. Miller's ailing sister every weekend, but if I see someone letting themselves into their home, it's the dogwalker they hired to take care of their beagle, Betty. Ruby hosts a poker game every Friday night with a couple of her girlfriends, and she invited me to come over for the next one. I gave her a half-assed answer, mentioning I might be busy, and her knowing grin as she glanced over at Jake's house was all I needed to know where she stood on the matchmaking front.

As for Jake... it's weird how I barely ran into him the first few months we both lived in Merrill Grove, but once I realized he was one of the mechanics at the garage where I brought my car *and* the young guy who moved in across from me, it's like I can't miss him.

I saw him at the grocery store two days ago, where he waved at me in between deciding what cut of steak he was buying for himself that night. I picked up a pizza the other day, and when I left the shop, he was coming out of the liquor store next door, carrying a six-pack, telling me with a grin he had the whole next day off and he was going to enjoy it.

And then, of course, there was the day he caught me checking out his fellow mechanic's handiwork, teasingly mentioning the garage's guarantee...

I don't get the vibe that he's into me. And while he doesn't have the same undeniable magnetism as my stalker, the casually friendly way he regards me is... refreshing almost. Like he'd be down if I gave him any sign that I was interested, but since I've been nothing but guarded since he introduced himself to me, he's following my lead.

He's safe. I don't know why he makes me feel that way, but I do. And the more he purposely keeps some distance between us, the closer I want to get to him.

Is that because I'm feeling a little put-out that my so-called 'obsessed' stalker doesn't seem as interested in me anymore? I'm not saying 'no', but I'd sure as hell deny it if anyone asked.

Doesn't matter anyway. I just got out of a bad relationship. Jumping into another one might be another mistake in a long line of them—but that doesn't stop me from calling out a friendly 'hi' of my own when I happen to be sitting on my porch one early June day just as he's walking out of his house.

He's not wearing his coveralls. I've noticed that, when he does, he's like Ruby: on his way to work. When he's in regular clothes—in this case, he has on a grey t-shirt, worn jeans, and a pair of brown boots— he's got a rare day off from the garage.

Instead of heading toward his car like he was probably going to, he jogs across the empty street.

I rise up from the porch.

Jake waves. "How are you?"

Wondering why he couldn't just wave from his property... "I'm fine. You're up early."

"You, too."

It's true. I had another nightmare about Will. Since I still don't know for sure what happened to him, I keep having this recurring nightmare about how he died. Last night, I dreamed that he fell into a pit of quicksand, cursing my name until it swallowed him up whole.

Do I really think that's how he died? Not at all. I

was afraid of quicksand when I was a kid, though, and since I've already gone through the usual suspects—a shooting, a stabbing, strangulation, *poison*—it was a matter of time before my wayward brain dragged quicksand into it.

What's next? Piranha?

I shake my head, clearing it. "It was a nice morning. Thought I'd get some fresh air before I hole up inside, maybe veg out in front of the TV. What about you? Big plans for the day?"

"You could say that. My mom needs my help moving some furniture around and building a new bookcase for my dad's study. Poor guy's useless with a screwdriver," he confides, a hint of humor in his tone. "I promised her I'd head over to Springfield to help as soon as I got a day off."

Wow.

"You're such a good guy— wait. Did you say Springfield? You mean like *Springfield* Springfield?"

"The big city about an hour away from here?" He waits until I nod, then says, "Yup. That's where I'm from."

"You used to live in Springfield? *I* used to live in Springfield!"

"Really? I spent my whole childhood living there. Downtown mostly, but my parents live on the West Side these days."

"That's so weird. We lived on the quieter side, out

in the 'burbs for a couple of years before I went to Connecticut for college."

"Connecticut, huh?"

"Yup. Graduated from Fairview University," I tell him.

"Cool. I went to school on the West Coast. California," he explains. "But I'm an East Coast guy. I moved back east at the beginning of the year, hanging out with my parents for a while before I found myself settling in here in Merrill Grove. But I still visit Springfield all the time."

For a second, I expect him to invite me to take the ride with him. I'd have to refuse, of course—no way in hell am I setting foot back in Springfield—but he doesn't.

Instead, he says, "Hey. I'd love to talk about this some more, but I promised my mom I'd be there by nine." Jake pulls out his phone, scowling when he sees the time. "I still gotta gas up before I get there."

"Raincheck, then," I tell him.

"How about dinner?"

I blink, a little stunned at the way he blurted that out. He didn't invite me home with him—that would've been way too damn much—but it looks like he finally decided to make some kind of move.

Didn't he?

I have to check. "What's that?"

"Dinner, Simone. You and me. I should be home by

five. Six at the latest. I don't know if you've been to Myrtle's, but she runs this great diner down the street from the garage. They have the most amazing soup and sandwiches. Ice cream sundaes, too. Why don't you let me take you out and we can finish this conversation later?"

We could do that here. Or, if he'll need to eat after he gets back, I could whip him up a sandwich in my kitchen. There's no reason for us to go out to dinner—but there's also no good reason for me to refuse.

I nod. "Yeah. Sounds like fun."

And that's how I find myself going on a date with Jake McIntyre—and wondering if my stalker will even notice...

TEN
WHO IS HE

SIMONE

wake up the next morning in the best mood I've been in in a long, long time.

I slept like a fucking baby. I didn't have a single dream, and I actually slept through the night instead of waking up randomly, reaching out for a body that wasn't there. No Will. No masked man who slipped into my bed as easily as he joined me in the shower... it's just me, and when I peer into the early morning sun, my room is just as empty.

I wait for Will to appear. To accuse me of paying attention to another man when he was the one I promised myself to, but no matter how I try to manifest him, I don't see him. I don't hear him.

And I smile up at my ceiling, thinking, *'til death do we part, asshole.*

Despite my inexplicable disappointment that I haven't heard from the Watcher since our shower, that's not enough to spoil the morning. There's a spring in my step as I start my day, getting dressed and peering out my window at another beautiful spring morning. The sky is a vivid blue with only a few whorls of clouds dotting it. The sun is shining brightly, and if the Watcher is out there somewhere, I hope he enjoys knowing that my dinner with Jake has put me in a fan-fucking-tastic mood.

He's cute. It's the best way to describe my neighbor. He's cute and he's kind, and I love that we have the Springfield connection. When he looks at me, it's like he knows me, like he actually *sees* me, but he's not expecting more from me than I can give him.

It was a friendly dinner date. We went dutch, got ice cream to go, and went home to our own houses. There weren't any expectations. No talks about tomorrow, either. Just a nice night out, and a morning where the guilt doesn't weigh me down first thing.

It'll come back. I wouldn't be surprised if Will isn't following me around the house by lunchtime, giving me grief for turning to Jake, but you know what? I don't care. He's dead. I got exactly what I wanted, and it's time he went to Hell because God knows that's where Will belongs.

But for as long as I can keep him out of my head, I'm going to enjoy it—and I get to do just that all the way up until I eat my breakfast, go outside to take a few moments to enjoy the gorgeous weather, then head over to my baby.

I'm feeling like a drive. Not because I'm tired of being haunted by the ghosts of my memories and my bad decisions, but because I don't feel shackled to them this morning. Why not taste a little freedom today, and if Will appears in my passenger seat, I'll know it's time to return to the house.

It sounds like a great plan to me. Who knows? Maybe I'll pick up donuts and see if Jake wants one...

I keep the top of my convertible up unless I'm actively driving my car. The doors are locked; unlike the night I let the Watcher in, I would *never* leave my car vulnerable. Nobody should've been able to get into my car unless they got their hands on my extra key. Of course, when I see what's waiting for me on the driver's seat, that might just be the case.

When it comes to my stalker, I wouldn't put anything past him...

No rose this time, and my stomach goes tight even before I pick the note up off of my seat. It gets worse when I see the block print and notice that he didn't sign it.

Wow. I must've really pissed my stalker off—and the tone in the four words seals it.

I guess I got his attention after all.

TONIGHT, ALL OF MY DOORS ARE LOCKED. I TRIPLE-checked my windows before turning in for the night. The shade in my bedroom is drawn. That door is closed.

Or it *was*.

It flings open with enough force that if my masked stalker didn't shoot out his hand and take hold of the knob before it crashed into the wall, I'd have a giant hole in it.

It's gotta be close to midnight. I went upstairs at eleven o'clock or so, putting my phone on the charger while I was reading an ebook on the Kindle app. Because I couldn't help myself, I did dare a peek out of the downstairs window earlier. Right before I changed into my pajamas and got ready for bed, I peeked out the bedroom window.

No one was out there. Not my dead husband. Not the hidden figure in the shadows, head tilted up, watching any silhouettes on my shade. If the Watcher was watching, I can't find him, and for another night, I convinced myself that he wasn't.

I still don't know where he could've been—but as I yelp and scramble out of my bed, my sleep shorts so loose and silky I nearly slip right out and face-plant on my floor—I know where he is *now*.

It's him. The Watcher. He's still wearing that strange mask that covers everything except for a pair of eyes blazing with intensity. He has on a pair of black pants that match his mask, the same inky-black t-shirt that's tight enough to show off his broad chest, sculpted muscles, and a coiled stocky body that looks primed to explode. His boots are on his feet, though the laces are undone.

I recover my balance, gaping at him. For whatever stupid reason, it's the laces that confuse me more than anything. Why is he walking around like that? Won't he trip?

I get my answer a second later. One powerful kick and the right boot is flying across my room, slamming into the side of my dresser. I jump right as he kicks off the left, careful to send it far away from where I'm standing.

I'm speechless. He's breathing so heavily, I don't think he can even spit out words.

Fuck. I don't even think I've seen him *blink* yet.

I'm watching him. He's watching me. Like there's a magnet pulling us together, keeping us connected, neither one of us can break away until he grips the bottom hem of his shirt and, in one practiced motion, yanks it over his head without disturbing his full-length mask at all.

His bare chest is heaving. Not an inch of hair on the baby-smooth skin, I notice. No scars, either, or a tattoo. It's perfect, deliciously tanned skin, and I'm instantly caught in his snare again—

—until I notice that, once his hands went back to rest on his thick thighs, he folded them into fists.

I shake my head. Okay. He's pissed.

He's really pissed.

"Who is he?"

Yup. He's pissed, and it's because he finally got the chance to confront me in person over my date with Jake.

Took him long enough.

I bat my lashes. "Weren't you watching? Don't you know?"

I'm nuts. Fucking insane. This man might not be that much taller than me, but he's got at least thirty pounds of pure muscle on me. Maybe more. So he doesn't have a visible weapon unless he's hiding one in his pants... through the streaming moonlight and the way he's bracing his legs like that, he's got something that looks like a lead pipe in there, but if he uses it on me, it's not going to hurt.

Much.

"Simone—"

"Watcher."

He growls. My masked stalker fucking *growls.* Looks like he doesn't like being called by a name that isn't his, even if he chose it himself.

I know what that's like.

Hey. He wants to call me his 'sweet vixen' even though I'm Simone? I don't know what his real name is since I don't know who he is. He calls himself the Watcher. He shouldn't be taking it out on me when I use that name.

He shakes his head the same time as he cuts his animalistic growl off. One step in his bare feet, then another as he moves into my room. "You know what I mean. I told you. That pussy is mine. You weren't supposed to touch it."

"I didn't."

That he doesn't try to accuse me of lying only makes me believe that my suspicion that he can see me no matter what is true. Just like what I said is. He told me not to touch myself. I haven't.

I give him a tiny smile that I'm not sure he can see in the darkness. "But you never said someone else couldn't."

He sucks in a breath, exhaling roughly. "You know damn fucking well that the only one allowed to touch you at all is *me.*"

"I do? Maybe you should've made it clearer, *Watcher.*"

"Simone..."

"Yes?"

"You want to test me right now? When I had to wait until it was dark enough to come to you to show you just how much you are mine?"

"I just wanted to make sure you still were keeping an eye on me. That you weren't busy with any other girl."

Under his mask, his jaw clenches. "Let me make this clear, baby. This is it. It's me for you. It's you for me. If you want someone touching that pussy of yours? You wait for me."

I shouldn't... I shouldn't...

"You're here now."

Did I mean to dare him? Tempt him?

Give him an open invitation to my body?

Who's to say—but that's exactly how he takes it.

Now, did I know that hitting it off with Jake would lead to my stalker finding his way into my bedroom? I can't say that I did—or that I'm complaining.

I should have been glad that the Watcher gave me some distance after our shower. I wouldn't put it past him to believe in the whole 'absence makes the heart grow fonder' bullshit, or to think that, the longer he left me wanting, the more I'd be grateful for a sliver of his attention.

Are there other girls? Is that what it is? He watches

me Mondays, someone else Tuesday, a third girl on Wednesday... If he's as possessive of me as he wants me to believe, shouldn't he have been back before now?

All good questions, but I find the words suddenly stuck in my throat.

I wanted his attention, didn't I? Because, one way or another, I've definitely got it now.

He's stalking me around the room. Keeping my eye on him, regarding him like a predator, like a wild animal on the hunt, I know I should stay still. Predators usually like the chase, and I'm the worst kind of prey.

I back up from him.

I can't see his face, but I can only imagine the shit-eating grin his mask is hiding when I run out of room. Instead of breaking for the door, I subconsciously—*consciously*—went the other way. I scooted back and back until, next thing I know, my legs have bumped up against the edge of my bed.

I trip. Fling myself? I don't know. He's still coming for me, his every step forward telling me that I could try to get away but that I would only be wasting both of our time, and before I know it, he's right there.

The Watcher's hand takes my shoulder, easing me back to the bed. He gives me every opportunity to resist. To shake him off, to kick him in his very prominent junk, to tell him I don't want this...

But *fuck*. I do want this. I'll probably regret it come

morning, but tonight? I lay back on my bed, running my hands over his warm chest as he follows me.

My stalker isn't an idiot. He has a woman spread out beneath him, so turned on because he managed to get past every one of her locked doors, including the bedroom. He has to want this. Has to want *me*.

I can see it in his eyes. I can feel it in the thrum of his heart beating wildly as his chest is pressed down to mine. His body weight is keeping me pinned in place on the bed, as though he's trying to make sure I'm not about to go anywhere.

I'm not. I'm ready for this, and I let him know with a soft, "Please…"

That's all I have to say.

He lifts up off of me just enough to grab my sleep shorts, pulling them off completely. A hiss escapes him when he sees that I didn't wear any panties to bed. After that, he doesn't bother with the top. A quick shove to bare my boobs to him is enough before he turns his attention to his jeans.

Less than thirty seconds after I murmured that one word to him and we're both wearing a single piece of clothing: my rumpled sleep shirt and his mask.

There's no foreplay. For my stalker, foreplay was walking around my room, the way I taunted him, and the way he chased. I already could tell he was aroused from the bulge in his jeans. He arrived like that, almost as though this was inevitable… and it probably was.

The idea of someone wanting me so badly that

they'd do *anything* to have me is such a fucking aphrodisiac. I'm panting softly, basically begging him to do what he said—to give me some relief—before he puts his two large hands on my inner thighs and pushes.

"Oh, yes. Baby… you don't know how long I've waited to see you like this. Your pussy is so pretty. So pink. I can't wait until I can spend the whole night worshiping it with my mouth like it deserves."

"Why… why don't you?"

He taps the bottom of his mask. "If I take this off, then I go. You don't want me to go, though, do you?" Dropping his hand, he dips his finger inside of me, gathering up evidence of how turned on I am. "Not when you need what my cock can give you."

I clutch the sheets beneath me as he spreads me legs as wide as they can go to allow him to wedge his hips in the gap. "Then what the hell are you waiting for?"

He grins. "For you to say 'please'."

"But I did."

He bows his body over me, shoving his cock all the way in with one powerful thrust. "I *know*."

ELEVEN
FOREVER

JAKE

My mouth waters for Simone, but the gentle mewl she lets out as I stuff her full with my cock... that sound alone is enough to satisfy any hunger I'll have for the rest of my life.

I didn't give her the chance to close her legs or think about what she was daring me to do. Her 'please' music to my ears, once I check and see that she's ready and willing to take me, I take *her*.

Seated inside of my sweet vixen, my fingers itch to reach the hem of my mask. I *want* her to see me. To know who owns her the same way that she infects every inch of my body. My heart beats for her. My lungs inflate because Simone exists in this world. If she didn't... then neither would Jake.

But she doesn't know Jake. She only knows the

Watcher, and the masked figure who lurks out her window, leaves her gifts and *himself* behind, claiming her entirely even before she bared that pretty pink pussy to his aching cock... he's the man she tempted into returning.

It doesn't matter that Jake got to sit across from her at the diner. Even as the small talk turned into something more, part of her was thinking about the other me. I had her attention in the moment, but the Watcher... he'd intrigued her. He captivated her.

And when I drew attention to the fact that she was taunting him by spending time with another man, even I could forget that we were one and the same. She used Jake to stoke the flames of jealousy within the Watcher—and thank fucking God I know Simone well enough to guess that that's what she's doing.

I would never force her. When I claimed this woman as mine, it would be because she's as addicted to me as I am to her. I needed her to ask for my cock. So she didn't spread her legs and say, *Fuck me, Jake*. She meant it anyway. I'm sure she did, and that's exactly what I'm going to do.

Only I have to remember that she wants the Watcher to fuck her. Nice guy-next-door Jake might earn her affection in time, but I'm tired of waiting. It's been months of watching her, stalking her, being so close but just not fucking close enough.

With my cock buried so deeply in her pussy, groins touching, her blond curls mingling with my pubes as I cover her body with mine, I don't think I can get any closer. That's not going to stop me from trying, though.

I leave my mask where it is. The time will come when I don't have to hide who I am anymore. Either because she'll fall for me so completely or because I'll do whatever it takes to make Jake McIntyre the perfect partner for her. I can be anything and everything for this woman, and if she needs a mask-wearing stalker to consume her, to take her, to *fuck* her and make her forget any man who might have come before me... I'll be *that*.

My fingers itch so, instead, I slip my hands beneath her sleep shirt. The material is silky, but when I get my palms on her tits, nothing is as soft and comforting as *Simone*. I'm still stretching her out, both of us panting now as I widen my stance, forcing her to spread her legs impossibly wider.

I've never seen anything more beautiful than the way her pussy lips are wrapped around my cock, leaving my shaft shiny when I withdraw from her heat the first time. I don't pull out all the way. I *can't*. Being inside of this woman is where I belong.

I also made it clear that this pussy belongs to me. If I don't want her to come to her senses and realize that I picked the lock on her back door, kicked open her bedroom door, waited until she'd stumbled onto the bed before climbing on top of her *and that she could stop me anytime she wants,* I need to show her why she *wants* to be mine.

And she is.

She is, and we both fucking know it.

I warned her. When I told her not to touch my pussy, and when I left the note behind asking about *me*. She had to expect this would happen. I tried not to take it personally that she locked the door tonight instead of leaving it open, but if she really didn't want me to find her in her room, why wasn't she wearing panties?

Simone knew she was mine—and now she is.

"How's that feel, baby?" I ask, slamming back home. The force of the thrust sends her sliding across the sheets. I tighten my hold on her tits, trying to keep her steady as I pick up the pace, developing a rhythm that makes it so I never actually leave her. "You like that?"

Her answer is to tilt her chin up, baring her throat to me like a sacrificial virgin on the altar. Her eyes are mere slits in her face, fingers clutching the sheets tightly as she grips onto as much of the mattress as she can.

"Harder," she pants, her voice so delicate and innocent that I can hardly believe she said the word. It's even better than 'please'. "I need... I need..."

"Oh, Simone. I know what you need."

I tug on her nipple. Pinch it. Tweak it. A tiny hint of pain to heighten her pleasure as I ruin this body. She's lifted her legs, hoisting them up, wrapping around me like some kind of spider money.

I thought I couldn't hit her any deeper. As she trades the sheets for my chest, nails digging into my skin, clawing me, *marking* me, I can't stop myself from rubbing my masked cheek against her flushed one. She might be beneath me, taking my cock like it's her communion, but there's no doubt in my mind that this isn't something that's just happening to her. That she's enduring.

Oh, no. Simone is fucking *me*, and it takes all I have not to nut the second I realize that.

This is why Will could never satisfy her. He treated her like a fucking sex doll, climbing on top of her, bouncing a few times until he got off, then rolling over when he was done. If that prick was feeling magnanimous one night, he might let her take the lead and ride him. He thought it was a treat for *her* to suck his cock.

I watched them. After getting a camera in their bedroom after pretending to work for maintenance, I learned how *not* to satisfy her. Same with the countless nights I obsessed over what she did in bed when she was alone.

Now I'm here. I have her. I'll pleasure her the way she deserves, and when my sweet vixen eventually goes to her knees for me, taking my cock between her lips, I'll worship her like the queen that she is.

Soon, I promise myself. For tonight, this is about making a statement. This won't be nice. It won't be gentle. It won't be anything that Simone deserves, or that will bore her. It'll be hard. Fast. *Passionate.*

It'll be a claiming, and when we both walk away from tonight, there shouldn't be a goddamn doubt about who belongs to who.

I made it my point to leave Simone wet and wanting when I left her in the shower. I checked the cameras religiously. Unless she snuck away to touch herself, she hasn't gotten any release since she was with me.

That was on purpose. I want her to understand that I control her pleasure. I'll deny her it—but when she's my good girl, I'll let her have it.

I'm dying to kiss her. On her mouth, on her tits, on her pussy. That's another thing I'll have to wait for since, to kiss her, I'd have to pull off the full-length mask. Soon, I promise. Soon I'll know her taste, and I'll find out what it's like to feel her tongue on every inch of me.

But that's not tonight. Tonight is about showing her that she's mine anyway I can.

She's squeezing me. Sweat slicks my forehead, drip-dripping down my back as I rock into her. Her soft moans tell me she's already close—as if I needed any other proof that her body is meant for mine. I'm possessing her, and she's seconds away from going off like a rocket.

Me, too, baby. Me, too.

"You're such a good girl," I tell her, only remembering to disguise myself in time. "I told you, didn't I? I told you not to touch my pussy. Look at it? So fucking hungry for me. You feel that? You're milking me, Simone. You want to take every drop I've got. And you will, won't you?"

She gasps. It's not actually an answer, but I decide to take it as a 'yes' anyway.

"And you will, won't you? Without anything between us, either. Just the way it's supposed to be."

No condoms. She's on birth control, we're both clean, and even if my stalking didn't reveal that all of that was true, I could give a fuck. I'll fill her full of me so damn often, she'll *squelch* when she walks.

From head to toe, I'm going to forever mark this woman as mine...

I almost thought she'd try to pull away as it hits her that she didn't even think to ask for a condom. She was always so careful with her *husband,* and here I am—

"Who... who are you?"

—and she has no idea *who* I am.

Soon, Jake. Soon...

I drop my head, pressing my sweaty forehead to hers. Can she sense it through the mask? Can she tell from the taut way I'm holding my body, pinning her in place, that I'd devour her if I could?

No one will ever separate us. Not the corpse of her husband. Not my family. She's it for me—and she's going to know it.

"Who am I?" I swivel my hips, changing the angle of my thrust as I pound into her again. "I'm *yours.*"

Simone gasps. At first, I think it's because of my

heated declaration. Then, as she clenches her pussy, coming all around me, I know that it's because I've caused her climax.

Her first climax.

Because me? I've waited too, too long for this.

And I'm just getting started.

THIS IS IT FOR ME. THIS IS MY FOREVER. I'M HOLDING IT in my arms, and after the way she welcomed me into both her home and her body, there's no fucking way I'll ever let go of it.

Of course, the moment I think that, she starts to slip away from me.

I tighten my arms.

She taps the top of my hand. "I have to go to the bathroom."

Fuck. I should've known that. She let me come inside of her, but I was a delusional fool if I thought she'd just lay there with her sticky thighs and my come dripping out of her.

My first instinct is to roll her onto her back and plug her up with my finger to make sure she doesn't lose any of me. It's pointless since I already know that one of the reasons why Simone didn't bother mentioning condoms is because she's on birth control. I've followed her to the doctors, heard her discussing different options before she settled on the shot.

I'm okay with that. Once, I thought that the ultimate sign that one of my girls was mine was getting her pregnant with my kid. Even if she wanted to escape me, if we shared a child, good luck trying to get too far away.

I've matured since then.

Simone will have my children one day. I'm not in any rush, though, and I'd like to keep her all to myself for as long as possible. It's my possessive instincts that fight back against her trying to get rid of me, but as much as it hurts me to let her go so soon after I had her, she asked so sweetly, I can't refuse.

Still, I give it one more try.

"Stay here. Let me—"

"No." She's firm enough that I know better than to push her on this. "I have to pee. Can I have privacy for that, at least?"

Getting laid makes me magnanimous. Opening my arms so she can leave them, I tell her, "Hurry back."

Devious little minx. She doesn't answer, but it seems like an eternity that she's in there.

Just when I'm sure that I'm going to have to go drag her back out again, the bathroom light clicks off, gentle footsteps heading toward the room.

She hesitates in the doorway. I can see her searching for me in the shadows, frowning as though she expected me to have taken the chance to slip out into the night while she was gone.

Or maybe it's the mask.

I refuse to take it off. Consider it hedging your bets if you will, but if she rejects the Watcher, I've got my foot in the door as myself. I got to see a different side of Simone when she allowed me to take her out to the diner by my job, and it only reinforced how addicted I am to her.

She's funny. Sly. Sweet, too, and generous. When I threw down a ten for the tip, she added a second one even though we had already split the bill, and it was barely thirty bucks to begin with. Smart. Devoted to her car which, to a guy like me, is a huge plus.

And she's fucking *gorgeous*.

Simone also managed to play perfectly into my waiting hands. For months, she never noticed Jake. She never noticed *me*. But as soon as the Watcher made his move, and then so did Jake, she teased one, then tempted the other.

Because that's what she did. Sitting across from me at the diner, looking at me as if she finally *did* see me... I didn't think it was possibly for me to want her more.

But she doesn't know that we're the same. For her to play with the Watcher in the shower, then go out with good ol' Jake to dinner, she was just begging my dark side to retaliate.

And, tonight, that was exactly what I did.

I'm not done yet, either.

I pat the space in front of me. "Come back to bed, Simone."

I'll put her there myself if I have to. If she thinks she's going to get cold feet and run now…

The bed dips as she lays out in front of me, giving me her back.

"I don't know who's crazier," she whispers into the darkness. "You or me."

Grabbing her by the hip, I pull her backward until I'm spooning her. Throwing my naked leg over both of hers, I trap her right where she belongs: with me.

Simone fits perfectly against my body. I bury my face in her hair, wishing I could give up the mask and breathe her in deeply. The fabric muffles the scent of her shampoo, her conditioner, and any trace of my come she's still wearing. I get tiny whiffs as I nestle my cock between her thighs, already so hard, it wouldn't take much for me to find my way inside of her again.

So why shouldn't I?

I hold her in place the same time as I grab the base of my dick. Lifting my leg up just enough so I can push hers apart, I trail my finger through her folds, checking to see if she can take me now.

I don't know for sure what she got up to in the bathroom, but there's not a drop of resistance as I slide through her moisture. She's so fucking wet. Just begging me to fill her up again.

And that's exactly what I do.

She gasps as I stretch her out, bottoming out with her ass against my groin. "Already?"

I bite down on her shoulder. Not hard. Fuck that.

I'll never cause this woman any pain, but the slight pressure from my teeth digging into her skin is enough to have her squeezing me tightly.

She rips a groan from my throat at the jolt of pleasure. Releasing her shoulder, I squeeze her hip, muttering in the Watcher's gruff voice. "*Fuck* me, Simone."

I didn't mean it as an order.

But she's doing just that. Rocking into me, fucking me softly, panting so beautifully, I nearly blow my load then and there.

I lick her skin, enjoying the tang of salt that hits my tongue. After pressing a kiss there, I selfishly let her pump me a few more times before I still her by grabbing her hip again, giving it a noticeable squeeze.

"Hm?"

"It's okay, baby. Just... relax. Can you do that for me?"

"Relax? With your dick inside of me? Is that what you're asking me to do?"

I love that she's not scared. The one thing in the world I don't want to do is frighten this woman. That she's hesitant and nervous—for damn good reason, too—but not scared... maybe I would rather just fuck her again.

No. *No.* I need the connection, and if she'll give me this, I'll give her the world.

I'll give her it anyway, but I still want *this.*

"This is where I belong. Where I've always

belonged. I told you. This pussy belongs to me, baby, and it always will. I filled it once with all the come I saved just for you. Now it's my turn to enjoy just how good you feel wrapped around me."

"So I just... lay here?"

"You keep me warm," I tell her, reaching around her so that I can cover her tits with my hands, completing the connection. "And I'll do that same for you."

She doesn't fight me. In fact, she arches her back just enough that there isn't an inch of me that she hasn't taken inside of her.

And then she lets out a wry laugh before she says, "I'm definitely crazy."

"Why do you say that?"

"You mean, besides the fact that I have conversations with my dead husband? I don't know. Maybe because there's a masked man in my bed with his dick inside of me," she reminds me. "He broke into my house. He's been watching me for weeks—"

"Months."

"Months," she echoes, her voice back to being a whisper. "I should be calling the cops."

She should. I'm not gonna deny that.

"So why haven't you?"

She shrugs, and though the way she moves sends another jolt of pleasure through me, I control myself. This is too important for me to get distracted with sex.

"I don't know."

She doesn't. I *do*. "It's because you know they can't save you from me. You're mine. They wouldn't understand our love—"

Simone's whole body tenses and, shit, her pussy is like a vice on my dick. "Love?"

"Yes."

I already told her. She didn't deny it in the shower. She only tested me on how well I knew her, and I passed that with flying colors.

You know what? My Simone doesn't deny it now, either.

Instead, without looking over her shoulder at my masked face, she asks pointedly, "Are you dangerous?"

"What do you think?"

"I think you know what happened to my husband."

Of course I do. I sent her that note, plus the ring. I made it obvious from the beginning that she didn't have to worry about him bothering her anymore. She got the message. Those conversations with her husband...

That's okay. She can talk to all the dead people she wants so long as I still get to call her mine. If she needs therapy, I'll take her. If she's happy to be crazy, I'm good with that, too.

After all, we both know I've got issues of my own, don't we?

Letting go of her left boob, I move my hand across her mattress, searching for hers. When I find it, I fold all of her fingers down except for one.

I'm sure she wants to ask me more about her husband. As I run my thumb over her ring finger, though, she breathes a little more heavily, waiting to see what I'm going to do—or say—next.

"Do you know how much I hated seeing you wear his ring?" I ask, my voice both gruff and conversational. "I like seeing it bare, but it'll look so much prettier when you're wearing my ring."

"Your... your ring."

"That's right. When I become your new husband."

"Because you got rid of my last one."

It's not quite an accusation. More a guess, but that's only because she doesn't know for sure.

"Do you want to know what happened?"

I can tell that she's torn. Part of her needs to hear it, while the sweet part of my sweet vixen wants to pretend like her lover isn't capable of doing what I did to her husband.

But I am. And if she's ever going to accept me as her next one—and she *will*—she needs to know just what sort of man she invited into her bed.

So when Simone finally nods into the night, I lay my hands on her shoulders, keeping her right in place as I press my lips to her ear and admit, "He came here thinking that he could take you from me... *hurt* you... so I slit that fucker's throat."

TWELVE
MUFFIN

'm in bed with my husband's murderer.

I fucked him, and when we were finished, I curled up next to him as he told me in graphic detail how Will died.

And all because he'd been watching me in Springfield, too, and he decided that he would be the hero I needed. I wanted a clean break from Will Burke, he figured that out for me, and I *got* it.

I also have the answer to the question I couldn't keep myself from asking: who's crazier? Well, one of us is a possessive stalker who killed my husband, and the other managed to fall asleep for a few blissful hours of dreamless sleep while wrapped up in a killer's arms as if they were the safest place in the world to be.

Oh, and she also routinely talks to the ghost of her dead husband when she isn't fantasizing over a masked man—or thinking about the friendly neighbor who lives across the street from her...

Will is dead. I know how he died now and I... I don't know. I feel better? I guess. Maybe. The Watcher wasn't brutal. Not really. Instead of making Will suffer, he slit his throat. It was a pretty quick death overall.

He doesn't tell me what happened to my husband after that. He makes it clear that no one will ever find him, explaining that the only reason he sent me the bloody ring was so that *I* knew Will wouldn't be coming back.

I want to believe that. I kind of do. I also think that he liked the idea of including me, of letting me know his murderous secret. No one else knows what happened to Will Burke except for us, and it's another way for him to think of me as *his*.

And after tonight? I am.

There was a promise in the way he fucked me. Even if he didn't tell me that I belonged to him, the possessive way he owned my body made it clear. First, when he was thrusting, then when he spent the next hour or so with his hard dick lodged just inside of me as if he never planned on leaving the warmth of my body.

But he does. Of course he does.

I should've known when he started thrusting into

me again. Light strokes, *loving* strokes, as he gripped my hip, backing me up into him.

I wasn't asleep then, and I'm pretty sure he knew that. This wasn't him trying to fuck me while I was unconscious. Oh, no. This is him showing me again that my body—just like the rest of me—belongs to him.

The moment he bucks up into me, filling me up again, I sense a goodbye in the way he slowly withdraws himself from me. Not wanting to face that... not wanting to face *him*... I close my eyes and pretend like I fell back asleep.

He slides across my mattress, trailing his warm fingers down my spine, over the curve of my ass before rubbing his thumb along the back of my upper thigh. I let him, still pretending to be asleep as he climbs out of my bed. I relax my closed eyes as he stalks to the other side, trying to keep up the illusion that I don't sense him prowling around my room while I'm even more vulnerable than when he joined me in the shower.

I don't know how long he watches me for now. True to his name, I can tell that he's there... just *there*... naked and masked and hovering at the side of my bed. I refuse to peek, to look, but just when I'm sure my stalker disappeared from my house as easily as he entered it, the floor creaks as his weight shifts.

He drops a kiss to the top of my head. He's still wearing his ski mask, the fabric rustling against my messy hair, but the gentle kiss is so at odds with his casual murder confession, I almost whimper.

Worse, I almost open my eyes, grab his wrist, and beg him not to go.

I don't. Not yet. Maybe if he had taken his mask off, revealing his identity to me, I would've. I can't fall for a mysterious, shadowy figure. I shouldn't be teasing my obsessed stalker at all, especially when I'm already so compromised.

I can't be with the Watcher, and I don't know what's going to happen when he realizes that.

So I stay quiet, my heart pounding in my ears as he walks soundlessly through my house. I can't quite make out his movements. He stalks away like he owns the place, like he takes locked doors as a challenge, and that he's sure of his welcome the next time I tease him.

Because that's what I've been doing, isn't it? First, I teased him by showing my naked body off against the window, snagging his attention. Then, whether I meant to do so or not, I threw my budding relationship with Jake in his face.

It was a dinner. One simple dinner. And as much as I enjoyed it, it did exactly what I thought it would.

It forced the Watcher's hand. He thinks my pussy belongs to him? That *I* belong to him? If he wanted me to believe that, he needed to show me.

And, whoa, did he show me.

What am I going to do about him? What am I going to do about Jake?

"What are you going to do about me?"

My eyes snap open. Even through the dim haze of the dawning sunlight streaming in through my window, I can spy Will leaning up against my dresser, sneering at me.

I grab my blanket, covering up my body as I sit up.

He snorts.

I get it. That was ridiculous for so many reasons. He's not real, I keep imagining him on my own, and even if he *was* real, he was my husband. He's seen me naked a thousand times. Nothing can change that.

Still, with my stalker's come still dripping out of my pussy again, and his scent clinging to my skin, it doesn't seem right to face his victim without something blocking my tits from my dead husband's narrowed gaze.

I know that face. I've seen that a *million* times—and it gets the same rise out of me this time as it always does.

"What?" I snap. "What are you looking at?"

"Let's see... how about the whore who slept with my murderer after he confessed to the crime?"

Well. He's not wrong.

I think about it for a moment. "*He* would've needed the extra large trojans unlike someone else I know." I wait a beat. "If we used them."

Will's eyes nearly bulge out of his head. "You let him fuck you without a condom? You never let *me* fuck you bareback!"

Yeah. Because Will wouldn't let me go on birth control. I'm just lucky he didn't poke any holes in our condoms or else I might've gotten stuck with his kid. I always wanted to wait until I was at least in my late twenties or early thirties before I tried to get pregnant, and while my high school boyfriend would've been happy to see me knocked-up at seventeen, Will agreed we would wait a few more years.

Still, I didn't trust him enough to go without condoms, no matter how much he swore we could do the pull-out method. With the Watcher... the first thing I did when I moved to Merrill Grove was find a GYN to prescribe me birth control. I'd like to think that a man this obsessed with me wouldn't risk my health by fucking me at the same time as he's fucking others— and I really, really hope I'm right otherwise I'm in even bigger trouble than I currently am—but even before I knew he was out there, I got on the shot.

And, with a gleeful grin, I tell Will that.

He hisses at me. "Don't you ever listen—"

I did. For far too long, I listened to him. "Go away, Will."

"Why should I? You did this to me." He moves away from the dresser, stepping into the light. For the first time since he's been haunting me, I see his second smile. A deep gash crosses his throat, the echoes of his dying blood trickling down his pale skin. "You killed me!"

Bile rises up in my throat. The afterglow from the second round of sex seeps away, replaced by nausea as Will gestures at his throat.

I swallow it back.

I knew he was gone. When he never came back to Merrill Grove after he tracked my debit card usage to the town, I knew something had to have happened to him. The wedding ring the Watcher left behind, plus his note, made it obvious. He had something to do with it.

Now I know exactly *what*.

He slit his throat, but he did it for *me*.

My tongue darts out, dabbing the corner of my mouth. I refuse to look away, and as I face the ghost of my dead husband, watching him begin to fade as I accept that the only one truly responsible for Will's death is *Will*... I give him a mocking smile of my own.

"You never should've hit me."

Shuffling into my kitchen after a few more hours of surprisingly peaceful sleep, I'm not sure what I'm expecting to find—or what I *hope* to.

The last time he slipped into my house, the Watcher left a rose and a note on my table next to the towel he borrowed. Before he left this morning, I heard the rustle of his clothing as he gathered them up, the way his shirt whispered against his chest as he pulled it on before stabbing his legs into his jeans.

I'm pretty sure he waited until he was downstairs to tug on his boots since I didn't hear those tapping against my floor. One of the chairs at my table is slightly crooked. He probably sat there to tie up the laces before...

...leaving me a muffin?

That's all that's left behind. I see a muffin resting on a napkin on the edge of the table. A quick sniff tells me that it's blueberry. Surprise, surprise that that's my favorite, and that the Watcher knew so.

I pick it up in one hand, reaching for the napkin in the other. He's trained me. I almost expect him to have left another one of his notes for me, but it's blank.

And it hits me. The fact that there is no message *is* the message.

Why would he remind me again that I'm his when he spent the last couple of hours proving that I am?

And if I'm his...

I slept with him. No denying that. He didn't force me to do anything, either. If I'd told him to 'go', he would've, but I didn't. I willingly climbed into bed with him *twice*. I wanted it as much as he did.

But what if I do want the Watcher, can I have Jake? If I choose Jake, how will my stalker react?

He killed Will. So he claims he did it for me. That he had a perfectly good reason.

With logic like that, what else can he convince himself that he's justified in doing?

I glance at the muffin again, then set it down on my table without eating it.

My phone's upstairs. Dashing to the second floor to grab it, I see that it's just after nine. If my neighbor's off from the garage, he'll be home. If he isn't, he might still be there since the garage usually opens at ten during the week.

I think about it for a moment, then search for his contact. During our dinner, he gave me his number so that I could contact him anytime, anywhere, if something happens to my car. To be fair, I gave him mine, though he hasn't called or texted me since.

And that, I think to myself, is exactly why I have to nip this in the bud before it gets even more complicated.

He answers on the third ring, my stomach going tight at the pure happiness in his voice as he says, "Simone! How are you? I was hoping to hear from you soon."

I'm sure he was.

"I'm good, Jake. But I was wondering... how would you like to go get some breakfast?"

I HAD EVERY INTENTION OF ENDING THIS... WHATEVER... possible *fling* I could possibly be having with my neighbor. It was just a little harmless flirting and a single dinner. I'll admit that most of my motivation had to do with drawing some kind of a reaction out of my stalker, and since I did...

I like Jake. More than I want to admit to myself. He's been so careful to come across as friendly so, the way I see it, why not tell him that we need to be just friends?

That was my reasoning behind seeing if he was up for breakfast. I could order sandwiches in, pick them up from a deli, meet him at Myrtle's, or even whip up some scrambled eggs. I've always been a big believer that it's best to break bad news over a good meal, and if that's because my dad took the family out to dinner every time he told us we were going to move, at least that makes sense.

Lucky me, but Jake got called into work today. He was actually supposed to be off, but the boss needed him to be in between ten and eleven. He told me he'd see if he could get Frank to let him come in later so we could grab a bite first, but I told him not to get in trouble with his boss over me. Instead, I'd bring him breakfast and, if he's not too busy, maybe we could have a real quick chat.

If I don't do it now, I'll back out. And I tell myself that as I get in my car, drive to the Merrill Grove bagel shop, and pick up breakfast.

I'm too nervous to eat myself so I order something for Jake, then head over to Frank's garage. I don't see

Jake's basic black car parked where the employees usually leave their vehicles. Only a white van and a beat-up dark blue pick-up truck.

A quick look around the front of the garage and the reception area reveals that the only one in sight is Brendon.

Where's Jake?

I've got the plastic bag holding a bacon, egg, and cheese sandwich plus a bottle of Coke in my hand, ready to ask Brendon where Jake is, if he had made it to work yet, when I see it.

At first, it looks like a scrap of black fabric. It could be nothing. It could be anything. Something about it, though, makes my heart nearly stop.

Brendon is underneath a tiny silver car, fiddling with it. He hasn't noticed me yet. Quickly, I tuck the plastic bag behind me, hiding it, before I tiptoe over to the... oh, who am I kidding? That's a ski mask.

A very familiar ski mask.

I poke it with the toe of my tennis shoe. The tip immediately finds the hole that's cut out for the eyes. I suck in a breath right as I bend over, picking it up.

My breath comes out as a shocked gasp loud enough to catch Brendon's attention.

Hearing me, he scoots out from under the silver car he was working on. His features are twisted in a look of annoyance at being disturbed, but he smooths them over the second he sees that it's a pretty blonde standing in his shop.

He doesn't get up, though. Staying on the creeper, he waves a hand at me. "Can I help you?"

Does he remember me, or am I simply one in a long line of female customers that he tries to sleep with? I don't know, and I don't care.

I show him the mask. "Is this yours?"

It would make sense. The car trouble I had. The way the Watcher was able to break into my car, plus my house. If he's a mechanic who knows his way around tools and lock picks... could it be him? Does Brendon own the balaclava and, unaware that I agreed to meet Jake here for breakfast, left it out by accident?

Is he my stalker?

I thought...

Brendon squints as he looks at the mask. "That? Nah. I know who it belongs to, though. Jakey. He works here, too. You—"

I don't listen to anything else he says after that.

This mask is Jake's.

It's *Jake's*.

Because Jake *is* the Watcher.

And everything I just thought about Brendon goes double for Jake McIntyre. Triple, when I think about how he just so happened to move into my neighborhood, conveniently renting the house *directly opposite of mine.*

Quadruple when I think that—

"Miss? Hey... you okay?"

Am I okay? The nice guy I'd kind of, sort of been

thinking about dating before realizing what a bad idea that would be is actually the mysterious stalker who killed my husband for me. Am I *okay*?

"Uh, yeah. I'm fine."

I'm fine.

I'm *lying*.

PART FOUR
DON'T YOU WANT ME

"YOU THINK YOU'VE CHANGED YOUR MIND

YOU'D BETTER CHANGE IT BACK
OR WE WILL BOTH BE SORRY..."

Don't You Want Me,
The Human League (1981)

THIRTEEN
HOME

JAKE

'm two hours into my shift, antsy and teetering on
the edge of losing my fucking mind.

Frank's doing payroll in the back office.
Brendon took off because he had a doctor's appoint-
ment as soon as I arrived. Another specialist, and I'd
feel a tiny bit guilty for it if I wasn't seconds away from
grabbing a hammer and taking my frustrations out by
banging on any part of the garage I could reach.

Simone never showed up.

She said she would. She offered to bring me breakfast, and I hauled my ass over to the garage as fast as I
could so that I wouldn't miss it when she arrived.

I didn't want her to be alone with Brendon. That
didn't end up being an issue since he was gone before I
even parked my car, but he got back about fifteen

minutes ago, bitching that his latest doctor can't figure out what's wrong with his gut.

I managed a few noncommittal noises, busying myself with tinkering with one of Frank's trucks. I'm pissed as it is that I had to come in today since we haven't had a single fucking customer yet. If Frank would've gotten off his ass to cover the garage while Brendon was out, I could be with Simone right now instead of wondering where the hell she is.

To add insult to injury, Frank's a bit of a hard-ass. When he's on-site, he refuses to let any of us use our phones while on the clock. I've seen him threaten a couple of other guys with their jobs if he catches them, and I need this job too much to risk his temper.

When he's not around, it doesn't matter. But when he's here... fuck. All I want to do is see if she's called or texted me. If I pull up the tracking app, I can see if either her car or her purse moved. It would take two seconds, but I can't spare them.

I slam my hand down on the side of the truck.

Brendon looks up from the paperwork he's doing. Once he figured out I wasn't quite paying attention to him, he found something to keep himself occupied. I want to ask Frank if it's okay if I head out since Brendon's back, but I know better. When the door to his office is closed, leave Frank alone. Until he does poke his head out, I have to stick around the garage with this guy.

He glances over at me. For a split second, he

frowns. His expression makes me think that he's trying to remember something he might have forgotten.

"Hey, Jakey?"

I'm usually so much better at controlling my emotions. *Usually.* But it's been more than two hours since Simone told me she would be stopping by to bring me a breakfast and maybe have a quick chat.

I know her. I know what she didn't say.

Something's up. Something's wrong—

"*What?*"

Brendon's dark eyes flash in annoyance. Grabbing something from the desk in the reception area, he flings it across the garage at me. "Just wanted to let you know you left this here yesterday. Must've fallen out of your coveralls or something 'cause it's not like anyone's skiing in fucking June."

A chill rushes through me even as my reflexes kick in, snatching the black *something* out of the air.

My mask.

What the fuck is Brendon doing with my mask?

I have three. I usually don't bother washing them, but after I wore it in the shower with Simone, I tossed this one in with the laundry.

Is he right? Could it have gotten caught in my coveralls and I didn't notice?

"Thanks," I tell him, trying to hold back the annoyance I can't help but feel. "I didn't even realize I'd lost it."

"You almost did. Remember that blonde chick with

the pink convertible who ghosted me? She stopped in earlier. She's the one who found it, too. Had to ask for it back before she took off without even telling me what was wrong with her car."

Simone didn't ghost him. My sweet vixen never had any interest in Brendon at all. He can be bitter as fuck all he wants, and I'd love to rub it in how there's nothing wrong with her car. The only reason why she was here was because she was coming to see *me*.

Wait—

She was here. Brendon saw her.

And Simone saw my mask.

No. *No*. She didn't. She couldn't.

Could she?

Fuck, fuck, fuck.

I don't care. Let Frank fire me. I only got this job because I needed to get close to Simone. But if Simone put two and two together and figured out that the Watcher's unique balaclava is *mine*... I have to make sure she's okay.

I have to explain.

Shoving my mask into the front pocket of my coveralls, I bolt toward the employee parking lot.

Behind me, Brendon's voice calls out, "Jakey? Where are you going?"

I don't answer him because I don't fucking know, do I? The second my ass hits the seat of my car, I yank my phone out of my coverall pocket. I try my best to ignore the pang that shoots through me when

I see there isn't a single damn notification from Simone.

It's okay. I have the tracker app.

My finger is sweaty as I try to open it up on my phone. I have to wipe my shaky hands against my coveralls a few rough times before I can get the touch-screen to work. When I finally do, I slap my steering wheel so hard that I nearly break my fucking wrist.

Because the tracker is offline.

Because Simone must have searched her car and found it.

Because she must have pried it off and crushed it with her wheels.

Because Simone is *gone*.

***

IT PAYS TO GIVE WAY TO YOUR OBSESSIVE SIDE.

When I was twelve, my parents already knew there was something wrong with me. My dad tried to insist that I was fine, but my mom was the one who brought me to be tested. Before I ever made it to high school, I knew that being so obsessive had something to do with my diagnosis: borderline personality disorder. I wasn't born with the ability to regulate my emotions, and I've spent the last fifteen years trying to figure out how to do it myself.

It doesn't always work. I fuck up, and that's how I lost both Casey and Heather. With Simone, I saw my third chance at forever. I've tried everything I could to make this one right, and that included being more logical than emotional.

Emotions told me that she'd never run from me once she saw how much I loved her. Logic said that I've already seen two girls be unable to accept the weight of my love. If Simone tried to leave me, I'd chase her, but I would never give her the chance to slip out of my reach the way that Casey did.

So I put a tracker on her car. It wasn't hidden too well because I didn't care if Simone found *that* one.

Not when I hit another in her trunk, and one in her purse. And that wasn't all.

If I could get my hands on a microchip tracker like I've heard the Sinners' tech guy makes, I would've shot it into Simone's arm while she was sleeping. Since I couldn't, I have to rely on the backup trackers, plus the secret app I installed on her phone while she was sleeping one night.

She thinks she can escape me. Once I get over my initial horror that she would try, I'm more than happy to prove her wrong.

The tracker leads me to a small four-story hotel about forty minutes away from Merrill Grove. My heart skips a beat when I see the pink Mazda parked in the lot. She has to be here. If it was anyone else, I might have thought they'd dump their car to throw me off the track, but this is *Simone*.

Her car is here and that means that so is she.

I pull off my coveralls, tossing them and my mask into the back seat of my car before I get out. I'm wearing jeans and a plain grey tee. Plain, boring clothes that you see on any guy around my age with the benefit that it doesn't have my first name embroidered on it.

I take a second to calm myself, schooling my features into a pleasant young husband who, whoops, was supposed to meet his wife here, but she has all the room keys now and she's not answering her phone. And, yes, I know it's not usual protocol to print me my own when she's the one who came in and rented the room, but you'll be doing me a big, big favor if you do…

Poor kid. The desk clerk is a fresh-faced brunette on the wrong side of twenty. Under my smile and my charm, she didn't stand a chance. With a hurried apology for even making me explain that much, she scurries off before coming back with a key card for Room 203.

Simone Burke's room.

You'd think she would've made up a fake name if she wanted to really hide out on me. There's no doubt in my mind that she *is,* and as broken as I am, one thing I'm not is delusional. She found out the truth about my identity too soon and she bolted, just like all the others.

But she's different. She's the one.

And I won't let her get away.

Even without the room number, I could've used the

tracker I have in her purse to find her in this chintzy hotel. Thanks to Amelia at the desk, I don't have to, and I take one last deep breath before using the keycard to let myself into her room.

And there she is. Standing at the hotel window, half-turned as if searching for something—or someone—as soon as the door swings in with the temper I couldn't hold back, Simone spins.

She gasps when she sees me. Not the Watcher, either, but *me*... "Jake. What are you... how did you..."

Simone didn't scream. No matter what happens next, the one thing I'll remember is that she didn't scream when she saw me striding into her hotel room. She gasped, and she took a few hesitant steps toward me, but she didn't scream.

That's my girl.

The ache fades. The tight ball that's been my gut this last hour... just looking at her has it loosening.

She's here.

I found here.

She's *mine*.

I close the door behind me.

She saw the mask. The way she's looking at me now... I didn't honestly think that she'd just decided to take a day trip out to the next city over for no reason. She knows. She knows I'm the Watcher.

And since she does, there's absolutely no reason for me to hide who I really am.

I point at her. "You left me."

My voice is shaking. It's nowhere near as deep as it is when I'm being the Watcher, but it's raw. In pain.

She *left* me.

Simone wasn't supposed to leave me...

She licks her bottom lip. "I went to the garage," is all the explanation she gives me.

"I know. Brendon told me. You found a mask—"

"Your mask."

I don't deny it. How can I? "Yes."

It's my turn to wait. To see if she's going to come out and ask me if I'm the man who burst into her room last night the same way I did just now.

Why would she? The answer to that question is right there. Mask or no mask, I can't hide who I am—and now there's no reason to.

But Simone... she's biting down on her bottom lip all of a sudden.

And I remember. That sensation that something was wrong, the nerves that have been fucking with me since she called and said we needed to talk. On my drive over, I thought, if there's one good thing that comes out of this, it'll be that she knows. She finally knows. I can be the Watcher *and* Jake, and whatever she wanted to say, she can let it go.

I don't think she's going to let it go.

"Why were you at the garage?"

I have a suspicion. It's twisted me up in knots all day, reminding me of that night when I realized that I was jealous of myself. I need her to choose both sides of me: the nice guy and the masked stranger who backed her into her bed before being invited into it.

But if she wanted one and not the other...

"Tell me, Simone. I need to know."

"Jake, I—"

I stalk toward her. She moves so that she's standing by the wall, one hand supporting her there while I rock back on my heels, desperate to touch her while also knowing that, right now, she needs me to keep some distance.

My heart stutters in my chest as all my worry from before comes rushing back. "Simone... Look at me. You've got me teetering on the edge. My sweet vixen... only you can do this to me. One word from you, and I'd fucking jump. Is that what you want from me? You want me to jump?"

The fingers on her free hand lifts up to her chin, covering her lips. She mumbles something.

"I didn't hear you."

"I said I went there to end things with you."

I go absolutely still.

"With me," I say, gesturing at myself. "Or me?"

I cover the bottom half of my face with my hand, a mockery of the balaclava I wore around her.

"With Jake," she confesses, and my heart fucking *breaks*.

I let out a howl of pain. "So you do want me to jump?"

She rushes toward me. "No. No! It's not like that. I

thought... I thought I was saving you. Right? That if the Watcher killed Will, and he found out about you... what if he hurt you? I had to let you go before I got too attached. That makes sense."

Her hands are on my arms, clutching me so tightly, her fingernails are digging into my skin.

"Listen to me. Okay, Jake? Listen to me. I can explain—"

Fine. "Then why did you go? When you saw the mask... when you *knew*... why did you run?"

She says she can explain, but she can't answer that with anything other than, "I don't know. I... I don't know!"

Her eyes are wild. No longer the sad, haunted eyes I love, something about the pure insanity in their depths now has me responding in kind.

Who's crazier: you or me...

Simone is here. She tried to leave, and whatever her reason, I found her. Always a planner, I had a backup in mind in case Simone reacted like this eventually, and I'm more than prepared to go ahead with it.

But first...

She's clutching my arms. I drop my hands to her hips, tugging her up against me.

The one downside to wearing a mask whenever I was with Simone is that I still haven't had the chance to kiss her. Not her mouth or her pussy, and I've spent months wondering what she would taste like.

The mask is off. Both of them are. With my fingers

a possessive brand on her hips, I squeeze her with just enough pressure to get her to gasp.

If I was Jake, I'd take my time, nibbling her lips, trying to coax her into opening up to me.

If I was the Watcher, I would've demanded her to open, then fisted her hair before kissing her.

Right now? I'm both, and the man that I've always been sees an opportunity and *takes* it. Her mouth is open so I slant mine over hers, just about fucking it with my tongue the same way I gave her my cock last night.

And because this is Simone... *my* Simone... she immediately responds to the kiss.

Suddenly, I have her hoisted up, legs wrapped around me, her back against the wall, fingers digging into her thighs.

And I'm kissing her as though both of our lives depend on it.

She's the first of us to draw away, and I follow her. Doesn't she know? Hasn't she figured that out yet? No matter where she goes, I'll be there, and it's the same right now. I give her a few seconds to breathe before I'm kissing her again, clutching her to me, trying to devour her any possible way that I can.

The kiss starts out forceful before quickly turning gentle. I get the chance to nibble, to taste, and I'm in fucking heaven—until Simone gets her breath back enough to speak again.

"You took off your mask, Jake," she whispers against my lips. "How do I get you to stop now?"

I want to tell her I won't. That I can't.

But as much as I'm obsessed with this woman, I love her even more...

"You tell me to stop."

"And you'll leave me alone?" Her forehead tilts until that's bumping against mine, too. "I couldn't get Will to leave me alone until I knew you killed him."

"For you, baby. I did it for you."

She sighs out a breath. "I know."

"You wanted me to."

She swallows roughly. "I did..."

"And now you're going to tell me that I'm the only one you've ever wanted while I fuck you and remind you that I'm yours, too."

Simone's eyes snap open. "Jake—"

"Should I stop?"

She opens her mouth. Closes it.

Shakes her head.

Thank fucking God.

Using the wall to hold her weight, I free one hand so that I can start tugging off her jeans. She braces herself with my shoulder, using her other hand to help me. We do the same with her panties, getting them down just enough that I have access to her pussy.

I lick my thumb, swirling it around her clit before dipping it into her pussy. She's so fucking hot, so fucking wet... I put my thumb in my mouth, laving off the moisture gathered there... so fucking *sweet* that I'm praying to every God there is and that's ever existed for her to say anything other than the word 'stop' right now.

To distract her, I bury my face in her neck, suckling it, kissing it, driving her mad to the point she's writhing with her back against the wall as I struggle with getting my own jeans down one-handed.

Almost there. Shit. The zipper's stuck. Come on... come on... *yes*.

The second I get my cock freed, I shift her just enough so that I can line our bodies up. One push. All I need is one push once I'm perfectly positioned and I'm right where I belong again.

I'm fucking *home*.

FOURTEEN

PART TO PLAY

SIMONE

He found me. I doubted he would. For all his words, for all his promises, when I took off, I was sure he'd let me go.

The only reason Will didn't was because I was spending his money. That's it. Sure, he believed he owned me, and I didn't mind that so much. I've spent my whole life belonging to *someone*. I'm usually happiest when I do because then I know who I am—who I'm supposed to be—and the part I'm expected to play.

The doting daughter who never gets upset or needs to be bribed to behave.

The goody-goody high school student who blossomed late, but found a boyfriend who adored her until she got too intimidated by his devotion, then escaped to an out-of-state college.

The perfect wife who stayed in the marriage because she was paid to, but who loved her husband's money far more than she ever cared about him. And who took the slaps, the name-calling, and the disgust so long as he paid her bills on time. But as soon as she had her second chance at true happiness, she threw his money in his face and left... only for that goddamn account to cause her former husband to chase after her.

Will didn't love me, either. How could he? You don't hurt the one you love, and you don't threaten to slit their throat just because they went on a shopping binge and spent a thousand dollars in two weeks.

Oh, no. But you do get your throat slit when you threaten a woman with a devoted stalker...

As Jake presses an open-mouth kiss to the place between my shoulder blades while spooning me from behind, I have to admit that he got it a little wrong. I'm *glad* he killed Will so that I didn't have to deal with him anymore, but that was before my dead husband started haunting me because I was a lot guiltier than I expected to be.

I didn't really expect him to kill Will. He never used to be violent; at least, not to me. There were rumors... who knows. His boyish smile and inherent charm concealed a dark side that called to mine even before I knew just how broken I was.

So I didn't expect him to kill Will, but I'd never been so fucking turned on in my life than when I received the note from the Watcher with Will's blood-covered ring. I knew. I knew then that Jake was still obsessed, would *always* be obsessed... and it was time I admitted that I felt the same.

He's here now. I made it as difficult as possible to test his resolve. The tracker I found ages ago got pried off with my fingernail before I drove out of Merrill Grove, but maybe he's better than I thought. It's possible he had a second one on my car, or some other way to track me down.

He even found my room in this hotel, and if I wasn't so flattered that Jake came right after me—instead of it taking *two fucking weeks* and more luck than he deserved for Will to find me—I might've been a little pissed that he got his hands on a key to my room.

Because he told me that he was my husband. Because he has every intention of making me his wife.

I glance down at my left hand, focusing on the naked ring finger.

It's about time I got a new one...

Jake gooses my hip. "Stay here."

He fucked me so boneless, I don't really feel like getting up. But I didn't think he would, either, so I roll onto my back, then prop myself up on my elbow just in time to see he's up and out of the bed, tugging his jeans on again.

We'd stripped after he banged me up against the wall. He was still desperate for me, and I needed him, so I brought him back to life with my mouth before climbing on top of him. It was my turn to take control —and he let me before his possessive nature got the best of him. My dark lover tossed me to my back, grabbing my ankle and pulling my leg over his shoulder so that he could fuck me impossibly deeper before collapsing on top of me once he'd finished with an undeniably possessive grunt.

Check-out isn't until eleven tomorrow morning. I'd planned on cozying up to Jake, rewarding him by spending the night with him before we sat down and discussed what would happen next.

This all happened because I couldn't be with both Jake and the Watcher. I loved his sweet side, I was fascinated by my stalker's darkness, and until he could come clean that he was *both*, we were both just fooling ourselves.

It's different now. Something's changed. Will's gone and Jake's here, and I'm finally—*finally*—ready to move on.

But what if he isn't? Is this like when he came to me as the Watcher both times before? He got off, got what he wanted, and now he's ready to just *go*?

My heart starts pounding. Praying like hell he can't hear it, I keep my voice light. "Where are you going?"

He checks his back pocket, nodding to himself as

he pulls out his wallet. "Saw a vending machine down the hall on my way over. I don't know about you, but I could use a drink." He pulls out two cards: his debit card and the room key that I'm still curious about. "They've got ginger ale."

My face breaks out in a grin. "My favorite."

Jake pokes his tongue in his cheek, raising his eyebrows. "I know, baby. I know."

***

WHAT THE…

My head is heavy. Woozy. It feels like someone took my brain out of my skull, stuffed some cotton inside, then plopped the top back on. My ears are ringing a little, too. And my mouth… ugh. It tastes like old socks with a hint of ginger.

My tongue is so dry that I come to, smacking it against the roof of my equally dry mouth.

It takes a second for my eyes to focus after I open them. I don't remember falling asleep at all, but the way my arms feel like deadweights as I shift against the stuffed furniture at my back, I'm sure I've been out for *hours*.

I must've been because how else can I explain waking up in a room that is most definitely *not* the hotel?

It's not my house, either. It's a living room, sure, set

up in a similar style as mine, with basic furniture that's not as comfortable as I first thought it was, but the walls are white instead of pink. No way it's mine.

So whose is it?

I blink my eyes a couple of times, then scrabble against the couch when I finally spy Jake standing with his back against the far wall, arms crossed over his chest, and attention focused solely on me.

For a split second, he reminds me of Will, but then he smiles that sly, possessive smile that's always warmed me up from the inside out, and I know that's not Will. It's Jake, and he seems pretty fucking pleased with himself.

What did he do? I don't remember falling asleep, but I do vaguely have a recollection of Jake coming back from the hotel hallway with two drinks in his hands. Both were open. The ginger ale was mine, the Coke his, and we sipped them together as we cuddled up in bed.

At some point, he suggested we go for a walk downstairs to grab dinner. I hadn't eaten in hours, but I wasn't feeling so great... and, as I squint, struggling to piece it all together, I do remember sleepwalking through the halls with him before everything went black.

Holy shit. "You drugged me?"

"Sorry, baby. I couldn't risk you sneaking out on me again. Until I've got my ring on your finger instead of Burke's, I'm not letting you out of my sight."

"And you *drugged* me?"

In my ginger ale. That has to be it. He got me a ginger ale and fucking drugged it so he could bring me here... wherever *here* is.

He doesn't lose his easy smile even as I'm shooting daggers at him with my gaze. "I needed you where I could keep you. If I told you I was taking you as my captive until you loved me as much as I love you, would you have willingly hopped in my car?"

I ignore that. "Where am I? Where's *my* car?"

Did he leave it behind at the hotel? I'll kill him—

"It's okay, vixen. Listen to me. I got your purse and your keys when we left the hotel. My car's still there, and I drove us home in yours."

My heart nearly stops. Yup. Still gonna kill him. "You *drove* my *car*?"

Jake chuckles as if this is somehow funny at all. "Simone, Simone, Simone... how can you ever doubt my love for you? What other kind of woman would be more pissed that I drove her car than that I knocked her unconscious so I could abduct her?"

He's not even a little wrong about that. "Fuck you, Jake—"

His dark eyes glitter. "Always."

I ignore that, too. "Where. Is. My. Car?"

"I parked it in my driveway. It's in perfect shape, and you can have it back when you say 'I do'."

Say 'I do'?

"You haven't even proposed to me!"

As if on cue, my obsessed stalker starts to drop to one knee.

I huff. "Get up. That's not funny. Where am I, anyway? You said your driveway... is this your house?" I get up, dashing for the window. I should be relieved when I see my house just outside, though I am when I spy my car sitting in his driveway, just like he said. "This is crazy. I want to go home."

I don't see him move. One moment, he was on the other side of his living room. The next? He's right there, grabbing me by the wrist, whirling me around.

I'm pissed. No. I'm *furious*. I'd worked so hard... *planned* so hard... and he's turned everything on its head by kidnapping me. Like he couldn't believe I might actually choose him, he once again took the choice from me—and now he's going to have to deal with the outcome.

"Let go of me."

"I'm not hurting you."

I don't care. "This isn't the way it was supposed to go."

His brow furrows. "What do you mean?" When I don't answer, he gives me a gentle tug. "Simone? You're closing me off. Don't do that. What are you thinking? Tell me."

I try to yank my hand back. His grip is gentle but too strong, and it's impossible.

That makes me angrier. "Get off me. You're a murderer!"

He rocks on his heels as if I hit him, though he doesn't let go of me. Not yet.

Instead, in a firm voice, Jake says, "You wanted me to kill him."

He's said that to me before, almost as though he's trying to convince both of us that his act of murdering William Burke was a gift he granted to me. He's not a killer. No. He's my *savior*.

If only he knew. But that's the thing. He *doesn't*.

He only *thinks* he does...

Jake angrily yanks out his phone. He jabs the screen with forceful fingers, swiping quickly as though searching for something in particular.

"You thought I was watching you from outside. And I was, baby. Nothing was more peaceful than sitting in the woods, crouching low, watching you through that window. But when I couldn't be there, that didn't mean my eyes weren't on you."

He gives me his phone. "There. Play the video."

"What's this," I ask, not even bothering to hide my suspicious tone.

As much as he did for me, I did *double* for him. For Jake, for the Watcher... and how did he repay me? Right when he proved himself, right when I actually believed that he loved me enough in his twisted way to always follow me like he promised... I gave him my body, and he gave me a roofie.

I trusted him. As much as I could trust anyone, I trusted Jake.

I've trusted him all along. Letting him into my house, into my *life*... letting him take the lead, knowing that he has to feel like he earned his prize, that he won long before he decided to stop hiding behind his mysterious alter ego... I did that, and he cheated by drugging *me*.

I'm done with playing this game. He thinks he's been a step ahead of me all this time?

Glancing past Jake, I look out into his empty room. I haven't seen Will since the night I stopped fighting my attraction to my stalker, and as I try to conjure him now, there's no sign of the ghost of my dead husband.

I got what I wanted. At least, I *thought* I did. But I wasn't looking for a killer. Not really. Didn't really appreciate a stalker, either, though I'd be lying if I said I didn't love the way it made me feel to have his eyes always on me like that.

No. All I wanted was my hero, and my happily-ever-after.

I worked so damn *hard* for it, and he doesn't know *any* of it.

He crosses his arms over his chest again. "The night the cameras picked up on you pleading with someone to get rid of Burke. He'd just banged on your door, promising to come back... and you said you wanted him dead. I did it, Simone. So don't you fucking call me a murderer. I did this all for *you*."

Without even watching the video, I hand the phone back to him.

He takes it, even as he wordlessly dares me to argue against what he said.

I don't, though I do grumble, "You think you know everything."

Jake's cocky answer is exactly what I expect from him. "I've made it my mission to learn everything about you."

I'd promised myself I wouldn't tell him. That he didn't need to know. If he got his kicks as the Watcher, I could be Simone... but, all of a sudden, I'm eighteen again, Jake McIntyre is looking at me, telling me that my life was his long before I had the chance to live it and... and... I *snap*.

"Okay. What's my name?"

I've caught him off guard. He takes a step back, releasing my wrist. "What do you mean?"

"My name, Jake. Because that's *your* name, right? Not the Watcher or anything like that. You're Jacob McIntyre. Jake's your nickname, and the Watcher is who you want to be. Come on. You know everything about me? What's my name?"

"Simone Burke." His face twists a little as he spits out Will's last name. "But you were Simone Walton first."

"No."

"No?"

"I changed my name to Simone Walton when I was eighteen. Simone for my great-grandmother. And Walton because I was crying in a Walmart parking lot the day I realized I'd have to change it if I wanted any chance of having a life of my own."

Jake doesn't even register that last part. I think he stopped listening after I mentioned the tears because anger bursts out of him, his face suddenly so hard, so *dangerous*, I feel bad for sicking him on my last husband.

"Why were you crying?" he demands. His hands are on my elbow, pulling me into him. "Who hurt you, baby? I don't give a fuck that it was, what? Nine, ten years ago? You tell me. I took care of Will for you. I'll get any bastard who makes you cry."

He still doesn't get it, does he?

"Who hurt me?" I break out of his hold, shoving him in the chest as my fury matches his. "*You* did."

Jake's eyes go impossibly dark. Instead of their usual brown, they're suddenly *black*. "Me?"

"Yes!"

"But... but..." Jake stops. I see it then. I see the sudden understanding dawning on him a split second before he drops his voice. "What's your name then?"

I hesitate. Something in the way he said that... he knows the answer. He just wants to hear me say it— and I'm not so sure I can right now.

"Jake..."

He shakes his head. "No. Your name. I told you. I've made it my mission to learn everything about you. I don't know your name." He takes a deep breath, and when he speaks again, it's so quiet, I shiver. "What is your name?"

There's no way in hell I can deny him this time.

"My birth name was Cassandra," I tell him, kicking my chin up in defiance. "But everyone called me Casey."

FIFTEEN
'TIL DEATH

JAKE

asey.

Casey.

I push away from the window, taking a few heavy, stalking steps away from her before whirling around, ready to accuse her of fucking with me.

I'd deserve it. After everything I put Simone through since I picked her out to be my final girl, the *one* I was gonna spend forever with, she should get the chance to fight back.

I stalked her.

Infiltrated her life.

Followed her to Merrill Grove, killed her husband, and made her my unwitting accomplice when I sent her the bloody wedding ring.

I messed with her car. Gave my co-worker repeated diarrhea so bad, he's going to a specialist now, all because he had the nerve to think he could make a move on *my* Simone. I left her flowers she couldn't explain. Notes that both threatened and titillated her.

I snuck into her house, snuck into her shower, snuck into her *bed*... I dominated this woman, not stopping until I had her completely under my control, and when she got her head out of the fog I created as the Watcher and made the smart decision to leave me, I proved to her that I meant it when I said that I'll never, ever let her go.

Fuck. I drugged her. Helped carry her out of the hotel before propping her up in the passenger seat, then drove her back to my house. *Our* house. I've finally lost my fucking mind, deciding that the only way to keep Simone was to lock her up where I could never lose her.

And now... now she wants me to believe that she's the first girl I ever loved? The one I did lose all those years ago, when I was young, dumb, in love, and had no clue to track her to *Connecticut?*

Because that's where Simone went to school. Where she met Will Burke, married him, and had a whole life with him until I chanced upon him yelling at her in Springfield.

I've always had a thing for blondes with sad brown eyes. When I saw Simone with the tears glittering in them, I was immediately drawn to her. I didn't know her name. Couldn't care less that she was married. She was mine, and I was prepared to do whatever it took to make it so.

I did the same thing when I was sixteen and Casey Mead was the new girl in school. I saw her trembling bottom lip, the worry in her haunted brown eyes, dreamed of running my fingers through her thick blonde hair, and knew I had to have her.

And I did. For a while. Casey was mine for two years before she started to pull away. I... didn't take it too well. I couldn't control my emotions back then, or my resolve. My obsessions were all-consuming, and I crumbled beneath their weight. I scared her. I know I did. She would bow her head, acting like my absolute need for her didn't frighten her to her bones, but I thought she understood.

I thought she loved me.

And then I lost her.

We graduated Springfield High together one day. A week later, she'd vanished, and no one—not her parents, not her friends, *no one*—could tell me where she'd gone. All I knew was that she got her first car as a graduation present, driving out of my life without ever looking back.

I had to let her go. Not because I wanted to, but because my skills at the time were good but not great. When Casey disappeared, she *disappeared.*

And now I know why.

Because Casey... is *Simone.*

I shudder out a breath, trying to make sense of it all. I suck in another, blowing it out through my nose. I fucking need control right now. If I scare her, if I send her running from me for a *third* time, I'll never forgive myself.

Her expression is guarded. I get the idea that she would've taken that secret to the grave rather than tell me the truth.

I'm so fucking glad she didn't.

Can you believe it? All along, I was pissed that Simone didn't recognize me from all the times I 'bumped into' her in Springfield. And Simone... *Casey* must've known that I was her high school sweetheart from the jump, and I had no damn clue.

A lump lodges in my throat. I swallow it with force, then peer into her face.

"Jake—"

"Shh." Don't scare her Jake, don't scare her... I drop my voice. "Let me look at you."

I've immortalized Casey Mead in my memories. Straight blonde hair instead of wavy, eyes the same shade of soft brown, with a rounder face and a different nose. There are some similarities between them, but could this really be *her*?

Casey was sixteen when she moved to Springfield. I was a hormonal boy with a broken brain. One look. That's all it took. One look, and I knew she had to be mine.

She wasn't my first kiss. That was Melissa Gordon. I

kissed her during a game of truth or date when I was thirteen, and it was so anticlimactic, I thought I was gay for a while. So I kissed Kevin Mitchell one night after a basketball game. That did shit for me, either.

Then I saw Casey holding her books to her chest, and I sprung a fucking boner right in the middle of history.

The first time I ever had sex, it was with Casey. Upstairs, in her pretty pink bedroom—

Pink. How the fuck did I forget about that until now? She loved pink... almost as much as Simone does.

I shake my head. "You don't look like Casey."

She lets out a soft laugh. "That's called aging, Jake." She waits a beat. "And, okay, a nose job when I turned eighteen."

I lift my hand, ghosting my fingers over the bridge of her nose. "Why would you change it? Casey... you had a beautiful nose."

"I did. But when you're a freaked-out kid driving her new car for the first time as you're leaving your possessive, overprotective boyfriend behind, you make a mistake and crash your car. Thank God I did more damage to my nose than I did my baby. Dr. Pavil could give me a nose job. If I totaled my convertible right after I got her, I never would've forgiven myself."

"Overprotective boyfriend? What? Me?"

The look she gives me could freeze water into ice cubes. "You're joking. Tell me you're joking."

I can't say that I am.

"You wanted us to get married at the end of the summer—"

"I loved you," I say simply.

"We were kids, Jake. You wanted us to be babies having babies when all I wanted was to go to college. And, yeah, we both know how well that turned out for me. Got my degree and a fucking MRS to go along with it, plus a husband who'd never let me use it. I tried to escape one overprotective guy only to get saddled with another."

Will fucking Burke. I have to swallow my growl at the reminder that Simone was married. But to think that, all along, it was Casey... *my* Casey... who slept in Burke's bed.

I didn't want to scare her, and I'm not so sure I pull it off when I whirl around on her again.

"If I was so fucking terrible, *Casey*, then what are you doing here? What am *I* doing here?"

Instead of shrinking away from me, Simone looks me in the face for a moment before she crosses the room again and sinks down onto the couch. "Because I never stopped loving you."

My stomach twists, sudden fury dying down quickly as her words. "What did you say?"

Her eyes meet mine and, fuck me, I see *tears*. "I was scared. I admit it. I was scared of a love as big as ours. So I ran, but you used to tell me that where I went, you'd follow me. Find me. That you'd never let me go."

Her lips purse and the tears become angry ones. "You let me go, Jake. You broke my heart."

"You changed your name—"

"Would that stop you now? If Simone became Lisa or Kathryn? If I got colored contacts next time instead of just a nose job? Would you give up on me then?"

Does she want me to?

Doesn't matter. There's something about her. There must have always been. I became obsessed with Casey when I was a boy, and the same damn thing happened again a decade later. Heather never loved me back, but Casey did once, and I'd hoped that Simone would now...

And she's telling me that not only are they one and the same, but that she never *stopped*?

"You know it wouldn't—"

That was obviously the wrong thing to say. Her hands fist the couch as she snaps, "So why was Simone worth the extra mile when Casey wasn't?"

Is that what she thinks?

"If I knew then what I do know, you'd never have been able to escape me. I would've found you. I always knew you were the one, baby. The *only* one. I tried to move on. It never worked. All these years, I think I've only ever been trying to replace Casey. If I could've found her, I'd do anything to show her that she belongs to me."

"Really?" She sounds like she's desperate to believe me. "What would you have done?"

I meet her stare dead-on. "I'd kill her husband because he made her cry, and because I knew that, with him gone, I had a better chance of making her mine. Then I'd watch her constantly. On my cameras—"

"I knew they were there. I had to constantly pretend not to notice them so I didn't tip you off."

I'm beginning to understand that. "—I still would watch her any way I could, from the cameras to standing outside in the wood because it has the best view into her window. And when she caught me watching, I'd send her a flower... and warn her that she was playing with fire."

"I like the burn," she whispers.

And that's why we've always been perfect for each other. "And then, when she finally admits to both me and herself that we're fucking soulmates, I would get my ring on her finger and ignore the fact that some other bastard had his there first."

"You were right, you know."

I like to think I usually am. But this time... "About what?"

Her voice is small yet determined. "I wanted you to kill him. I've spent years regretting that I let him talk me into marrying him when I knew I still regretted leaving you first. When he moved us to Springfield because he knew that the entire fucking city reminded me of you... I don't think I could've hated Will more in that moment. And then..."

"And then?"

"You came back for Christmas." Her lips twitch, a hint of a smile taking the place of the earlier frown. "And the Watcher became the watched."

The watched... like she was watching me? No one *ever* watches me. I hide in the crowd. I rarely stand out. I blend in so seamlessly that it makes it so damn easy to stalk any of my targets.

I join Simone on the couch. "You want to run that by me again?"

"I told you. You thought you knew everything. But did you know that I waited until we were in the Springfield Shop together last December to pick a fight with Will? Just so you could see how poorly he treated me?

"When you started coming around in all those disguises, I knew you hadn't changed one bit. Jake McIntyre and his need to save me... you didn't even *know* it was me, but there you were." Simone starts ticking off on her fingers. "The guy with the petition and the hat. That was a good one. Bringing up our food. Oh, and the time I bumped into you in the elevator and you pretended you were moving in even though everyone knows that building was rent-controlled and no one ever left."

Huh. Well, that explains why I could never get off the waitlist—

Wait.

"You saw me? You knew it was me?"

She pats my knee. "Every time. It was only when

you had your mask on that I wasn't sure. I was hoping you were the Watcher... I'm sorry, but that's just a very Jake McIntyre thing to do." Bumping her shoulder into my bicep, she teasingly adds, "Your penmanship's got a lot better over the years."

I don't... I don't get it. If everything she is saying is true...

"If you wanted a second chance with me so bad, why didn't you tell me? Why did you run?"

All of her humor flees as quickly as it appeared. I instantly regret saying anything, especially since all I needed to hear was that *Simone loves me*, but I did— and she actually answers me.

"Because I needed to know that, this time, you *would* follow me."

How could she doubt I would?

"I had a tracker on your car—" I begin.

"I know. I found it and flicked it off."

I know that. "But you didn't find the second one." I reach down, taking her hand in mine. "Or the one I hid in your purse."

She blinks up at me in surprise. "That's how you found me?"

"That's two of the ways," I confess. "And if I had this tech ten years ago, you never would've gotten away from me in the first place. I love you. Nothing's changed for me. I still want you. And if I have to lock you in my house—"

Simone rises up, shifting in her seat before

throwing her arms around my neck. As she squeezes, she says softly, "Your house. My house. I don't give a shit. I'll stay with you as long as you promise to always, always come for me."

If that's all my sweet, cunning, conniving vixen needs, I think I can manage that.

Did I think I was obsessed with this woman before? She manipulated me. When no one else did, she *saw* me. She used my love for her to get what she wanted: her husband gone, his money free to claim, and her high school sweetheart panting after her as if we were both sixteen-year-old virgins again.

I thought I was stalking her, following my plan… but she's the one who was the puppetmaster the entire time.

Shit. If she wasn't drawing away from me so hesitantly now because of my stunned silence, I might just throw her back on the couch, claw off her clothes, and show her just how fucking hot I am knowing that she pulled all of that off with me being completely oblivious.

I might still do just that, but before I do, I need to set my future bride's mind at ease. "Try to leave me. Next time, I bet I break my record."

That erases some of the sudden worry from her eyes. It's not enough, though. She has another question ready to fall from her lips, and I'll answer it if she needs me to.

I'll do anything for her.

I wait, and after a moment of silent encouragement, she shudders.

"Do you love me, Jake? Can you still love Simone?"

If that's who she wants to be, I'll love her just the way she is.

"I thought I knew what love was. What obsession was. And then I met you, and it made me doubt everything I've ever known. I loved Casey, but I love the woman Simone's become, too. And now that I know you're the same... it all makes so much fucking sense."

"Oh, *Jake*..."

"You've always been the one. And," I tell her, slipping my fingers through hers, clasping our palms together so that we're connected, "we always will be together."

'Til death do us part.

EPILOGUE

FOUR MONTHS LATER

SIMONE

Jake might not need to watch me from the shadows now that both of our identities are out in the open, but that doesn't stop my new husband from doing it anyway.

Nothing excites him more than catching me doing something when I think I'm alone. Considering our co-dependent relationship means we're rarely apart except for when he's at work and I'm busy in our house, I make sure to take a few moments every day to give himself to watch.

He's my Jake, but I hope he never stops being the Watcher.

It's easier these days. Frank's rule of the guys down at the garage keeping their phones tucked out of sight while they're on the clock went to hell after the day I tested Jake's dedication to me. He would've rather lost his job in order to chase after me, and when Frank tried to discipline Jake over it later, he pulled on that boyish grin of his, shrugged, and said something about being sorry that Frank had to fire him, but he wouldn't apologize for having to run out when he had a family emergency.

Right. Because even when I was hip-deep in trying to get him to recognize me, to see *me*, my old high school sweetheart was already convinced that my new self was his.

And then the truth came out, he learned that I used to be Casey before I was Simone, and he was so eager to lock me up before I changed my mind and left him again, we were married at the Merrill Grove court-house the second week of June.

Frank didn't fire Jake. Of course not. My husband is one of the best mechanics in the area and he works cheap; to get close to me, he needed the garage and didn't care about the rate of pay at the time. He doesn't need money. With Will's healthy bank account enough to keep us comfortable for a long, long time, he could work if he wanted to, or quit and stay at home with me around the clock.

He called the old man's bluff, though, and when Frank backtracked, Jake got a raise *and* the muttered assurance that he could use his phone whenever he needed to.

So Jake stayed on at the garage. I teased him that he did because his deep-seated jealousy had him keeping an eye on that shameless flirt, Brendon, and while Jake didn't even try to deny it, he told me that he felt better about sticking around the garage because it gave him access to a shop where he could easily tend to any issues my Mazda convertible might have.

Like, seriously... how can I *not* love this man?

The hours apart while Jake's at work is good for us. Over the last couple of months, I've devoted myself to turning my rented house into a home for the two of us.

We decided to stay in mine. My landlord was more willing to discuss selling the house to use instead of renting it, and we celebrated closing the deal a month ago with a night out in Springfield, where we went on a double date with Jake's older cousin, Royce, and his new wife, Nicolette.

Jake introduced me as Simone. Though I'm sure a part of him will always think of me as Casey now that he knows the truth, I purposely shed that image, my past, and my family the day I left Springfield in the first place. I changed my name. I got the nose job after my accident that completely changed my face. My parents divorced shortly before graduation. My mom remarried a few years ago, my dad's workaholic tendencies caught up to him and put him in an early grave, and I knew there was something wrong with me when the only person from my old life that I missed was Jake himself.

I loved him. At sixteen and seventeen, it was puppy love, and I thought I would get over him. When I met Will shortly after moving to Connecticut, I used him to try.

Then I saw my Jake in Springfield last winter, and all the old feelings came back. Casey loved him—and so does Simone.

I'm in the spare bedroom, a paintbrush hanging loosely in my hand. I threw my hair up in a messy bun, though a huge chunk of it fell loose earlier, falling into my face. Instead of fixing it, I keep batting it away. The result is that I'm pretty sure I have a mauve streak of paint on my cheek, but I was determined to finish painting this room before Jake came home for dinner.

I'm wearing an old, oversized t-shirt that belongs to my husband. It keeps slipping off of my shoulder. There's paint on the dark fabric, too, but after working my way through most of the house, I've gotten to be a pro at keeping the mess to a minimum.

When I sense someone sneaking up behind me, my heart lodges in my throat. I know it's not Will. My dead husband hasn't haunted me since the day he blamed me for killing him, and I stopped pretending I was faultless.

I wanted him dead. I'm glad he's gone. I'm sorry that he was collateral damage in our love story, but when Jake slips into the room, his hands landing possessively on my waist before nuzzling my throat, I'm not sorry that he had to die for me to get the happily-ever-after I deserved.

It could've been Will. I was too afraid of how much Jake thought he loved me—too sure that I didn't deserve it—and I settled for another man. It could've been Will, and if I'd never seen Jake again, it might have been.

But I did, and as I toss the paintbrush into the paint pan, squealing as I turn around in his arms, throwing mine around him, I can't bring myself to regret anything that happened.

We've been married for almost four months. I keep thinking that the shine will wear off, that our honeymoon period won't last forever, but as Jake ducks his head, kissing me 'hello', the thrill rushing through me says that it hasn't yet.

It's early. I wasn't expecting him for at least three more hours. I wait until he finishes kissing me—and I finish kissing *him*—to ask him about that.

"Aren't you supposed to be at work?"

His dark eyes twinkle. "I told Frank I had an emergency at home."

"Oh?" I ask, not bothering to hide the slight tease in my suddenly breathless voice. "And what was the emergency?"

"The emergency was that my gorgeous wife sent me a video of her fingering herself, telling me that she needs her husband's cock."

I did that while I was waiting for the first coat to dry so that I could make sure I liked the color before I committed to a second coat.

I give him the slightly wicked grin that has Jake moaning and calling me 'vixen'. "I could've waited until your shift was over."

"You could've, baby." He grabs my shorts by the waistband, tugging me so that our bodies are flush. Even so, he muscles his hand between us, slipping it past my shorts, finding his way into my panties. "I couldn't."

Another thrill rushes through me; this one is a combination of anticipation, lust, and *want*. Only—

"Wait—"

Jake raises his eyebrows, finger already gently nudging my clit as that deceptively boyish grin has me just about creaming myself already.

I go up on my tiptoes, giving him more access to the rest of my pussy even as I shake my head. "Not in here," I gasp as his thick finger breaches my entrance, filling me all the way up to his second knuckle. "The paint's still wet."

We learned our lesson. The last time Jake came home for a lunchtime quickie and a little dessert while I was in the middle of painting the downstairs bathroom, he decided to bend me over the sink basin, banging me while we both watch in the vanity mirror. That was okay—and then he got the idea to hoist my naked ass up on the counter so that he could go down on me to help me finish faster.

And boy did I, but I also ended up the with dark pink paint streaking my hair, my cheek, and my neck after I started writhing around on his face.

"So?"

"So, I just did the second coat. I'd really like to not waste my time doing a third."

He glances at the wall. "You did a great job in here, baby. Looks good. I like it. That painting you got the other day's gonna look great, too."

A man who appreciates my effort, who compliments my taste, *and* doesn't mind that I spent a hundred and fifty dollars on a single painting for the spare bedroom... and who just hefted me up in a bridal-style carry to bring me to our room down the hall all because he respects my work?

Like I said...

How can I not love this man?

But I do. I always have—and I always will.

JAKE
THE WATCHER
silhouette
SIMONE
THE ONE

AUTHOR'S NOTE

Thanks for reading *Silhouette*!

While this is a standalone, it is a part of an extended universe. Royce's story delves deeper into what actually happened between him and Heather, and you found out just what went on when Nicolette went missing! Keep scrolling/reading/click for a sneak peek at that book, as well as what's coming next.

I also want to let you know that, if you purchase a physical copy of this book—paperback, discreet paperback, or hardcover—please send me your name and mailing address via email (carin@carinhart.com) and I'll mail you a free *Silhouette* bookmark and a signed bookplate for your collection!

xoxo,
Carin

THE DEVIL'S PLAYGROUND

ROYCE

Link called himself a sap once. For mooning over Ava when she was in a relationship with another man… but he still wanted her. He held out hope he'd get his second chance with her. And while I'm sure he'd prefer she didn't have to go through what she did for him to have it, he's happy with how everything turned out.

Me? I don't know what will come of my obsession with the gorgeous waitress, but I can finally say I get what Link meant. Because I haven't even been able to be with any other woman since the moment I met Nicolette, and I've never even *had* her. At least Link had memories of his Ava to keep him going on the lonely nights. I just have my hand, my wry attitude, and a couple of photos kept hidden on my phone.

I shake my head, trying to knock out just how

fucking pathetic I am. Then, knowing this is unavoidable, I give Link my trademark winning grin. "Okay. You wanted me to stop by to see you. What's up?"

"Right. Got something to talk to you about."

"I'm listening."

Link clinks the bottom of his shot glass against the tabletop, the liquor sloshing slightly. "Jake."

Shit.

I knew it.

Keeping my tone light, I ask, "What did my cousin do now?"

What *won't* Jake McIntyre do?

"Did you know he was back in town?" Link asks.

I can't lie to him. For one, he'll know and get pissed. For another, I respect him too much to even try.

"He called me a couple of weeks ago. Mentioned that he met another girl—"

Link throws back his head, groaning loudly. There's a reason he chose this booth to claim for his infrequent trips to the Playground. Not only is it shadowed, giving us privacy, but the acoustics here are amazing. Despite how loud the crowded club is tonight, I can't pretend I didn't hear Link's groan—or his obvious annoyance in the sound.

I hold up my hand. "I know. I *know*—"

"I know you haven't forgotten what shit he pulled the last time he 'met a girl'."

A lump lodges in my throat. I swallow it roughly. "No. I haven't."

"If it wasn't for Jake… look. I know what happened with that other girl was a mess. A fucking disaster. But if Jake had listened to what you told him, it wouldn't have been our problem. You understand?"

"Yeah, Link. Of course. What? You think I like cleaning up after him and his messes?"

"Why not? Since that girl got killed, you've been cleaning up all of ours."

Ouch.

It stings double that he's not wrong. A guilty conscience is a bitch, and I've spent the last six years trying to find a way to smooth mine over. When Heather died… Jake took off. I gave my aunt and uncle some money to send him to a college on the other side of the country so that the fallout from her death didn't touch him. He was just a kid—barely twenty—and he had no idea that falling for the wrong girl would end up with the Dragonflies and the Sinners on the brink of World War Three.

Link smoothed it over without any other bloodshed; at least, not more than could be expected when a Dragonfly's sister dies in the arms of one of his enemies. Knowing that Jake was out of Springfield helped, and I figured he'd want a fresh start in California.

And then, at Christmas, he visited home and told me all about Simone Burke, the most recent woman that caught his eye—*in Springfield.*

You think I'm obsessed? That's nothing compared

to Jake... and maybe that's another reason why I finally decided to give up on Nicolette. When my cousin tells me the lengths he goes to catch Simone's attention... at least I just followed her in my car.

Jake? He'll sprawl out on the backseat of his target's...

"I'll take care of him."

"We can't fuck up this truce, Royce."

As if I need a reminder of that. "We won't, boss. I promise. Don't worry about Jake. I got it."

"I know you do." Link takes his first sip of whiskey, a sure sign that the hard part is over. I grab my shot, scooting it toward me as he pointedly changes the subject. "Okay. Now, about that DB you guys cleaned up last week..."

In the Devil's Playground, a Sinner always plays to win.

NICOLETTE

I needed money, and I needed it *fast*.

When my job as a hostess at the local Italian place

wasn't going to earn me enough to cut it, I did the one thing I promised I would never do: I got involved with one of the syndicates that rule Springfield.

Considering I'm trying to avoid anyone with ties to the Libellula Family, I head to the West Side, and hope like hell the Sinners Syndicate will give me a chance.

The Devil's Playground isn't my first choice, but what else can I do? I make it clear that I'm only interested in serving drinks... until some big shot gambler offers me ten grand for one night.

I take him up on it—only to have him wager his night with me to another guy... and *lose*.

Now I'm expected to honor my deal with the Syndicate's underboss, and the charming bastard who hired me for this job in the first place... while also hiding any ties I have to his enemies.

ROYCE

From the moment Nicolette walked into the Playground, I wanted her—but then I brought her on as one of our girls, and she was suddenly off-limits.

I learned the hard way: work and pleasure don't mix. If I'd met her anywhere else, I might've taken a shot at the waitress, but she needed the job more than she needed a boyfriend, so I backed off.

And, okay, that's a damn lie. I didn't pursue her, but hell if I didn't take a page out of Devil's book and start watching over Nic from the shadows...

I would have left it at that, though, until one of the Playground's more well-known wallets set his eyes on my girl.

They don't call me "Rolls" for nothing. I played him for the night she agreed to, telling myself that I was just saving her from what the sick and twisted customer wanted to do to her.

Then I get my first taste of Nicolette, and I realize that one night will never be enough... and I'll stop anyone who tries to take her from me.

The Devil's Playground is the second book in the **Deal with the Devil** series, a collection of interconnected standalones set in the fictional crime hotspot of Springfield. It tells the story of "Rolls" Royce and the one woman he'll do anything to save, Nicolette Williams.

SAVANNAH

Five years ago, the Libellula Family ruined my life.

It doesn't matter who was responsible. I blamed the man who created his gang of thugs: Damien Libellula himself. If it wasn't for him giving free rein to his soldiers to pass their funny money through my store, I wouldn't have been accused of money laundering—and counterfeiting.

I was a naive twenty-five-year-old then. Four years in a minimum-security prison later, and I'm out for revenge.

I changed my name. My hair. My accent.

My *life*.

And I did that all because my plan to get revenge on Damien? I'm going to stalk him. Infiltrate my way into his life in any way I can. I'm going to make him trust me.

Maybe even love me.

I'm going to seduce him—and then I'm going to kill him.

At least, that was the plan. But Damien, he has a different one.

Before I can do any of that, he makes me his *wife*.

DAMIEN

I thought it was amusing at first. The gorgeous

brunette who followed me everywhere, too stunning to hide in any crowd.

Then, when I grew impatient to see what it was she wanted with me, I approached her—and she stabbed me in my side.

Another man might be put off by something like that. Not me. I've always liked my women feisty, and Savannah's murderous side was so refreshing in a world where everyone bows down to me.

At that moment, I decided I would do everything to bring her to her knees.

Following a page out of my old rival's book, I made her a deal: she goes back to prison—and that's assuming she survives my Family long enough to be charged for attempted murder—or she gives up her freedom and becomes my bride.

I know she only chooses the second option because she thinks she can get close enough to kill me again.

I must say, I'm looking forward to her trying... especially when I'll certainly enjoy showing her just why she shouldn't.

Dragonfly is the third book in the **Deal with the Devil** series, a collection of interconnected standalones set in the fictional crime hotspot of Springfield. It tells the story of mafia leader Damien Libellula and the one woman who will trade revenge for something more, Savannah Montgomery.

Releasing June 18, 2024!

KEEP IN TOUCH

Stay tuned for what's coming up next! Follow me at any of these places—or sign up for my newsletter—for news, promotions, upcoming releases, and more:

CarinHart.com
Carin's Newsletter
Carin's Signed Book Store

facebook.com/carinhartbooks
amazon.com/author/carinhart
instagram.com/carinhartbooks

ALSO BY CARIN HART

Deal with the Devil series

No One Has To Know *standalone

Silhouette *standalone

The Devil's Bargain

The Devil's Bride *newsletter exclusive

The Devil's Playground

Dragonfly

Dance with the Devil

Ride with the Devil

Reed Twins

Close to Midnight

Really Should Stay

www.ingramcontent.com/pod-product-compliance
Lightning Source LLC
Chambersburg PA
CBHW060349310726
48976CB00003B/765